PRAISE FOR

GONE
MISSING

"Can curiosity be a blessing and a curse? In the little-known place called Cinder Bottom, Smokey and Do What will bring you along on a fun adventure filled with mischief and mystery, all spurred by one young man's insatiable curiosity."

DANÉT PALMER, author of *Baptized by Love*

"*Gone Missing* is an intriguing historical fiction mystery, adventure, and coming-of-age story that will have readers enthralled until the end. Based on real-life accounts from life in the heart of Appalachia, it tells the story of two fourteen-year-old boys that find mischief, conspiracy, and danger in their small town of Cinder Bottom already known for scandals."

HEATHER LEE DYER, award-winning author of the *Zodiac Drift* series

"*Gone Missing* is an action-packed tale about young Smokey and his sidekick, Do What, set in 1958 Cinder Bottom, a red-light district nestled in the hills of West Virginia. When a federal agent comes to town, the duo use their street smarts—and cunning—to enlist a cast of colorful characters to help them untangle the truth about the stranger's identity and whereabouts. Drawn from real-life stories, this page-turning mystery will delight would-be detectives everywhere!"

LAURA WHITFIELD, author of *Untethered: Faith, Failure, and Finding Solid Ground*

"Set in a West Virginian coal hamlet aptly named Cinder Bottom, *Gone Missing* takes place against the backdrop of the Brown v. Board of Education court decision that roils segregated schools. Cinder Bottom homeboys, fourteen-year-old Smokey and his buddy Do What pair up as sleuths to solve the mysterious disappearance of the area's US congressman and the sudden appearance of other strangers in Cinder Bottom. As the boys work to unravel the mystery, readers will enjoy the cast of local characters, from the Italian grocer to the madam running the brothel that serves as a halfway house for young women fleeing abusive conditions. The story appeals to YA and adult readers, spiced with social critique and a wholesome appreciation of the major characters. (Note: a sequel is on the way.)"

CECELIA TICHI, award-winning author and
faculty member at Vanderbilt University

"This book is captivating, engaging, and delightful! I can hardly wait to learn what happens in book 2 and book 3. The characters in the *Gone Missing* story grabbed my heart, and I kept turning the pages to see what Smokey, Do What, and their friends would do next. I've not spent much time in Appalachia, and this book made me want to go visit."

MARI RUDDY, bestselling author of *Extreme Healing*

"A captivating journey from start to finish. *Gone Missing* is a powerful coming-of-age story. Part mystery, part action-adventure, and a cautionary tale about the secrets that small towns can hold. I didn't want it to end."

KIM KARPOWITZ, editor and author of *Decode Your Darkness: Give Your Emotions a Voice and Heal from Childhood Trauma*

GONE MISSING

ADVENTURES IN CINDER BOTTOM **1**

GONE MISSING

STEVE VANNOY
AZUL TERRONEZ

Rockrose Press

An imprint of AUTHORS WHO LEAD™

Paperback ISBN: 978-1-954801-72-1
Dust Jacket ISBN: 978-1-954801-90-5
Case Laminate ISBN: 978-1-954801-92-9
eBook ISBN: 978-1-954801-90-5

FIC043000   FICTION / Coming of Age
FIC066000   FICTION / Small Town & Rural
FIC002000   FICTION / Action & Adventure

Cover design and typesetting by Kaitlin Barwick
Edited by Lauren Woodbury and Melissa Miller

cinderbottom.com

This book is dedicated to the loving memory of

"SMOKEY" CURTIS VANNOY

and to all those who call West Virginia home.

CHAPTER

1

Ed Farmer had four boys. All had reddish-blond hair except for Jacob, whose hair was jet black. Jacob had been born while Ed was in the penitentiary for an unpaid moving violation that he refused to pay.

None of them Farmer boys had jobs. They were moonshiners, and that was as good of a living as anything in McDowell County, West Virginia.

Smokey—a fourteen-year-old, dark-haired boy whose stature was more like a man's but who had the innocent face of a boy—made his way up to the Farmers' to buy a quart of liquor. He was buying it for a regular get-together he had with his not-so-bright but loyal friend Johnny "Do What" Bailey. He got his nickname because no matter what you asked of Johnny, his response was always, "Do What?"

Do What lived up the holler from Smokey and had been in school with him since the second grade. Both of their fathers worked in the coal mines.

The Farmers lived just past Burke Mountain outside of Keystone and Northfork, two of the bustling coal-mining towns nestled in the heart of the Appalachian Mountains. They had moonshine stills hidden in several strategic locations; this made them difficult to find but easy to destroy if the law happened to be on a hunt.

The local sheriff, Donnie, didn't bother with the Farmers' business. When he did get a whiff of trouble brewing in the air, he would track down one of the Farmer boys and ask them what Ed was up to this time.

Smokey knew where the stills would be hidden. He knew they needed to be near a source of freshwater, so they were likely to be near a spring. The stills had to be up a holler so that no stranger or hunter would stumble upon the hidden operation. Finally, they had to be as easy to set up as it would be to abandon so that if they needed to, they could burn down the operation.

Smokey and his gang, on more than one occasion, had been to the stills but left them just as they found them. They didn't want to risk the punishment they might face for stealing; even a dip from the still could mean a beating or worse.

Smokey and Do What would often hunt these stills for fun. They had drawn out a treasure map of just about every single one in the county. While Do What and Smokey shared similar simple dispositions, they did not share the same smarts.

Smokey was both street smart and book smart but paid little attention to school. He kept up his grades so he could play baseball.

Do What was neither book smart nor street smart but was as loyal as they come. He would stick up for his friends and stand at attention at the first sign of trouble. Smokey liked that about Do What. He appreciated that what his friend lacked in intelligence, he more than made up for with his devotion and commitment to the small group of friends they called brothers.

Smokey told Do What that he would use his paper route money to get the moonshine and that he could chip in once he sold the rifle he had been trying to hawk to old man Jenson for the last month with no luck. Smokey figured Do What would be trying to sell that old rusted good-for-nothing rifle for ages.

Smokey noticed the eldest Farmer son, Jacob, leaning on the back of his truck. He had the rear tire jacked up so that if the law wondered what he was doing, he could say he had just been changing his flat tire. Smokey was uneasy. He'd rather be dealing with Billy; he was his age and they played ball together on occasion. Jacob was sour to speak to and always seemed to be ready for a fight. Though Smokey was close enough to be seen, he wasn't acknowledged by Jacob at all.

The wind rattled the sycamore trees as it gusted gently through the holler. The warm afternoon air settled over the treetops.

Jacob was bowlegged and had a large scar near his eye, partially covered by his black hair. The scar was deep and prominent and gave him the look of a villain who had been scorned. The rumor was that his father gave him that mark for burning a batch of moonshine when he'd fallen asleep while they were still cooking the sugar. The scar made Jacob look like he might come unhinged at any minute and the menacing grin he carried left you with an eerie feeling that he might be destined for a shady future you didn't want any part of.

Smokey walked up and leaned on the rear bumper of the 1946 rust-colored Chevy next to Jacob.

Without looking in his direction, Jacob asked, "How many do you want?"

"Gimme two quarts," Smokey said, intending to give one to his pa and one for the brothers, and handed him the money in change.

Jacob counted it and reached into the cab of the truck. He grabbed two quart mason jars and handed them to Smokey.

They exchanged a few words about baseball and then said their goodbyes. Jacob wasn't much for words and, rather than spoil the semi-pleasant exchange, Smoke immediately left with his jars stuffed in his shoulder sack.

The Farmer family provided a good deal of moonshine to Cinder Bottom, the notorious, yet hushed about red-light district in Keystone. Cinder, or the

Bottom, as it was simply called, wasn't far from Dead Man's curve along Route 52. Despite the small size of the town, Cinder drew a steady stream of men looking for liquor and ladies. The Farmers moonshine business was just one of many. They weren't the only shiners in the county. It was important, in fact, for there to be several outfits in operation; at any time the law would take one down.

The crackdowns would happen whenever a bigger judge was up for election or a new politician wanted to make a name for themselves. They liked to say how they had destroyed the devil's brew at local churches to win points with Holy-Roller voters. Everyone knew that these raids were just stunts to make headlines. Cinder Bottom was too important of a red-light district to actually close it down.

Those who visited Cinder Bottom from the outside came for three reasons: to drink, to gamble, or to find the company of a lady. Sometimes they came for all three. It was a town built during the height of the coal boom of the late 1800s. It served as a place for the wealthy, the clergy, and politicians to have the anonymity they required for their secret acts where no one would say a word. It was an unspoken rule that what happened in Cinder Bottom stayed in Cinder Bottom.

Those who lived and worked in the area had an understanding that no one would ever reveal the identity or the activities of the visitors. They had a small but prosperous life despite their remote location and sometimes hard circumstances.

Cinder in the 1950s was a place that had experienced racial integration for many years; there were both colored brothels and bars that were frequented by both whites and blacks. Some married white men from the larger cities in the northeast would make their way to Cinder to find a young black prostitute to lay with and to enjoy the freedom not to be judged or bothered.

Big Ma ran the most infamous colored whorehouse in Cinder and ruled her beer joint like a well-oiled machine. She sold beers for a nickel and had the jukebox playing with the latest music. There was no sign for Big Ma's place. The cinder block exterior, weathered paint, and dusty windows made her place seem almost abandoned. The entrance was in the rear and, once you entered, it was as if the outside world stopped.

Smokey and his gang were welcomed there to have a beer but were seldom given any access to the back rooms where the girls would wait and then bring their johns to the back for a spell. Smokey and Do What had even gone to the back once to help Big Ma paint one of the rooms. The room was nearly empty except for a lonely bed and a small nightstand where the only lamp in the room stood.

The room they painted was dark and smelled musty. There were no doorknobs on the doors but the holes were still there and on occasion, the boys had tried to peek into other rooms. Despite their best efforts, the dimly lit rooms revealed nothing but squeals.

The main room of Big Ma's featured a long wooden bar cluttered with ashtrays and a can to make change for the jukebox and call for a girl. Dim lights behind the bar cast soft light on the hazy room and lit the faces of the patrons, both regulars and newbies. They would chat as they guzzled their drinks and waited for their turn. During the daytime, Big Ma had Ernie the bouncer grill out on the back porch and serve sweet tea to her girls in preparation for the evening.

Ma was seldom seen during the day. She was ashamed of the horrible acne that scarred her round face. She preferred the soft light of the bar at night. You could see how beautiful her features must have once been. The scars seemed to reflect the life she had led—her beauty had faded long ago. Her plump figure still had the shadows of her youthful curvy body. Sometimes, she could be found dancing at the end of the evening when the patrons had finished the liquor and the girls were done for the night.

Big Ma was kind to Smokey, offering him odd jobs here and there to make some extra cash. It made him feel important. He honored the code of Cinder Bottom, and Big Ma knew he could be trusted.

Smokey stashed his liquor in his jacket and headed to the makeshift baseball field at the edge of town to meet Do What to partake in a bit of moonshine before they headed to the Hatler house, where the weekly Friday night gathering of the brothers occurred.

The house was once a company home that miners would rent from the mining company. There had been a time when miners had no other choice but to live in the company houses. The only homes you could rent in the Holler were owned by the company. The money they earned was spent at company stores and went right back into the company's pocket.

No matter how hard someone worked as a coal miner, they never could seem to escape the company. Though the pay was better than any other job in the county, it was impossible to scrape enough cash together to get out of McDowell. The miners' lives were closer to indentured servitude than paid workers. Workers could have a nice stove but they had to work years to pay it off. Most folks just succumbed to the life the company meant for them to have. They learned to be happy to have a job, a roof over their heads, and food to eat.

Many of the miners were immigrants or descendants of immigrants like Smokey's family, who had escaped the hard life of the farms of North Carolina to the city life that places like Northfork, Keystone, and Welch had to offer. The dust-covered, black faces of the men that filed out of the mines each evening were always a bit more worn down than they had been the day before.

By this time, the miners led a less prosperous life than the one that lured them to the mines from the farms years ago. When Smokey's father had come to McDowell County, he had been drawn in by the running water and electricity in the company houses, luxury not afforded on farm life. Over time, the hard life of working in the mines had dulled the lure of modern conveniences.

Smokey knew that the long-drawn faces of his father and friends were not a sign of hope but a trap that he never wanted to be a part of. He vowed that if he could find a way out, he would.

Smokey remembered that he needed to drop off the other quart of moonshine to his father. He had used his paper route money to buy both quarts of liquor—one for his father and one to share with the brothers. He never asked his father for money to buy his moonshine, but on occasion, his pa would give him a few half dollars and tell him to keep the change so that he would have some walkin' around money. Smokey figured the least he could do to repay him was the gift of some firewater in return.

When he arrived home, he presented his father with the quart of moonshine and watched as he took a long drag from his cigarette. He motioned for Smokey to set the quart jar on the railing.

Smokey peered at his reflection in the window and ran a comb through his already slicked-back dark hair before making his way off the porch. His father, whose face was still covered in soot from the mines, called to him.

"Smoke!" he hollered from the back stoop. "Go help your mama put away those potatoes in the root cellar before you go."

Without questioning, Smokey hurried around to the cellar and hauled the twenty-pound sack of potatoes down to the root cellar. He hated going down there. The cellar was dark and wet, but the real trouble was the memory that surfaced each time he stepped down the stairs. It haunted him like a monster under a child's bed. He had only been five at the time of the incident, but he had never forgiven himself.

He dropped the potatoes and hurried back upstairs, slamming the cellar doors shut as if to trap the memory once again in the darkness. He rushed back to his pa and told him he was going to hang out with Do What and he would see Pa in the morning after his paper route. His father, a man of few words, didn't even gesture. He continued to stare into the distance, as if he was longing for someone to return. Perhaps he wanted to return to the hard but pleasant life of the farm.

Back on the old family farm in North Carolina, people made daily pilgrimages to fetch water from the natural springs. The waters were said to have incredible, magical healing properties for those who were afflicted with all kinds of ailments. Smokey's Aunt Annie, who lived a simple primitive life on the family farm, had never married. She treated her farm, her animals, and all her kin as her own children. She was a wiry-framed woman with a grip of a sailor and a mouth to match. She reeked of tobacco, which she grew and dried herself, and of goose feathers from her handmade feather bed.

Smokey had fond memories of visiting Aunt Annie every summer. The solitude of her farm seemed to protect Annie from the progress of the world that advanced around her. She still fetched her water from the spring each morning before firing up the wood-burning stove to cook and make her coffee. She didn't seem to enjoy the simple life as much as she seemed to belong in it. No matter how much her kinfolk wanted to provide her with more modern conveniences, she always reverted back to the simple ways of her youth. The electric stove that Smokey's dad and bothers installed sat unplugged like a piece of furniture. She refused to use it and relied on the woodburning stove for heat, even in the coldest of winters.

Annie reminded Smokey of the simple times that his family must have once enjoyed before the mines, before the mine company had arrived and began to rip the coal from deep within the earth.

Those simple days were long gone for McDowell County, and the idea of returning to such a rural simple existence was never a consideration of anyone in coal country, though the life of the miners was hard. At least their kids could attend school and have a chance to get a better wage.

Smokey was one of the few boys his age that had a proper job. He'd had his paper route for almost four years, ever since he was ten years old. He inherited it from Do What's older brother who had left for the Navy. He had tried to give it to Do What, but he could never remember the route or the houses or would forget to collect the monthly fee for the papers and thus lost his paycheck to cover the losses. Do What figured that if he gave the route to Smokey, then he could enjoy the Friday evening liquor run and at least get some of the benefits that the paper route provided.

Smokey didn't mind the job so much; he was able to get some exercise and visit with a few friends along the way. It kept him busy after school and provided $1.75 a week, just enough for his moonshine and a quarter for a few snacks during the week. Smokey dreamed of bigger things, but the paper route would do until he got a real job one day, far from the mines.

He never told his father about his dreams. He feared that his father would think that he didn't believe the life of a miner was good enough for him. He appreciated his dad's hard work, but he also remembered the day they received the news that his grandfather had been in a mining accident. A slab of stone had fallen on him, breaking his back. He lived hunched over now, constantly in pain.

Smokey knew his grandfather's lungs were as black as his father's face after a shift at the mine. He feared that his dad might die there, a fate that he never wanted to have for himself. But for those who lived in McDowell County, it seemed inevitable that the boys would grow up to work in mining in some way or another; there was nothing else to aspire to. Going back to the farm was seen as a step backward. No one would ever consider that, no matter how hard it was there in the coalfields.

Smoke waved to his father, who finally acknowledged him with a raise of his now three-quarters-full quart of moonshine. Smokey scurried off before his mother asked him to do more chores. He wanted to play ball in the field with his friends as he did each week but worried his mother would ask about his chores. It would be a stretch of the truth to say that he had completed them. She didn't approve of his sneaking around and didn't like his habit of smoking and would have a fit if she knew he was drinking all night as well.

Smokey could see Do What heading down the road, so he picked up the pace to meet him.

They walked on the shoulder of the main road that passed through Keystone to avoid the careless drivers that wandered too close to the faded solid yellow line. Smokey liked walking with Do What because he observed the strangest of meaningless details. He would stop and ask Smokey if he noticed the way the leaves seemed to be dancing when the wind howls.

Today, Do What's gaze was fixed overhead.

"Smoke, have you ever wondered why the sky seems like it never ends?" he asked.

"Ah, hell, Do What, how in the heck would I know? I think it's something about the gases that form the atmosphere," Smokey said.

"Man, you are smart, Smoke. That sounds right," Do What said.

These kinds of questions intrigued Smokey. Do What wasn't like his other friends; in fact, Do What was often the butt of the joke among the rest of the brothers. Smokey never let it go too far and would cut them off if they got out of control. Some fun was fine, but he didn't want to see his friend hurt, and when he had enough, he let them know.

It was on these walks to the field that Do What seemed to cherish the most. He was such an old soul. It was like he was an eighty-year-old freshman. An old man in a kid's body. He often forgot things and didn't really have any other true friends besides Smokey, which suited him fine.

As they rounded the last curve before they were at the baseball field, they saw an unusual sight.

Ahead of them, the sheriff had pulled over to the shoulder. He was speaking with a man in a fancy Thunderbird, definitely not from around Keystone, but maybe a car from the regular visitors from bigger cities coming to Cinder Bottom to have a weekend of fun.

As the boys approached, they noticed that the sheriff and the man were not having a casual conversation. Smokey quickly grabbed Do What's arm and pulled him into the trees off the shoulder.

"Hey, why'd you do that?"

"Shh, quiet or they'll spot us," Smokey barked. He led them around the road, heading up toward the tree line where an old deer trail followed the road.

When they got close to the sheriff and the stranger, they crept quietly toward the cars. They crouched in silence, straining their ears to hear.

"Naw, I ain't seen anyone like that here in Keystone," said the sheriff.

"Now, are you sure you haven't seen anyone with that description?" the man asked.

"I told you what I know and I know everything that goes on here, who's coming and who's going, and I'm telling you I haven't seen him," the sheriff answered. "Besides, what did he do that you Feds want him so bad anyway?"

"That, sir, is official state department business."

The man handed the sheriff his business card. He stared at it, unsure what he was supposed to do with it.

"Call me if you hear or see anything," the man said. "This is a matter of great importance. We need to find that man, but you mustn't involve anyone else, you understand? We need your cooperation in this investigation."

Sheriff Donnie liked the idea of being on the inside of an official investigation. He was used to the Feds coming to hunt out moonshine stills to prove that no illegal liquor would be tolerated. These raids were more of a statement to the bosses back in Washington than a real investigation. This seemed different. Something about the man's tight lips told Sheriff Donnie that this was serious business.

"Yes, I understand," the sheriff said, wiping the sweat from his brow. He felt like he was being questioned by his high school principal. The man said nothing further, turned around, and headed back down the road away from Keystone.

The sheriff raised his hat and scratched his head, looked at the card, then tossed it on the ground, and got back in his police car. He drove off toward Keystone.

Smokey waited to be certain the two cars were out of sight, then he headed to the road to fetch the card.

"Hey, Smokey, wait for me," Do What said, hurrying forward to see what he had discovered. "What does it say?"

The card had the official state department seal, and the name "Max Tucker, Agent on special assignment" was printed on the card with a phone number.

Smokey stared at the card. Something didn't seem right. Why would a man from the state department be looking for a man in Cinder Bottom? Who was he looking for? And what had he done? They were too far away to hear the full description of the man, but Smokey had managed to hear something about the man being blond with blue eyes.

"Let's keep this between you and me, you hear?" Smoke said sternly.

"Do What?" Do What was already looking up at the trees, looking at the outline the leaves made when the sun shone through them.

"Do What, don't tell anyone about the sheriff and that man, you understand?"

"Oh, yeah, got it. You can trust me, Smokey. I won't say a word."

Smokey knew that Do What was trustworthy, but he worried sometimes that he would slip up. Sometimes Smokey felt he was just plain dumb and knew he had to be specific about what he agreed to.

"Don't mention the car, the strange man, and the sheriff. Got it?" Smokey ordered again.

"Got it," Do What answered. "Can we go now, and can I have one of your cigarettes?"

Smokey was always willing to share if he had extra and he handed him a Pall Mall he had stolen from his brother's secret stash in his sock drawer. He had hiding places for just about everything: cigarettes, moonshine, and dirty magazines. Smokey knew all of the spots. He knew that his bother would never confront him; if he did, he knew he could be ratted out.

It was an unspoken rule that Smokey would take two cigarettes a week, not more.

Smokey struck the match, lit both cigarettes, and handed one to Do What. They wandered down the road to meet the brothers. They walked in silence, taking long drags on their cigarettes, but Smokey's mind was racing. Who was the strange man, and who was he looking for? What had he done?

When they were almost to the baseball field, Smokey began to wonder if the man really was ever in Cinder Bottom. What if this man wasn't in trouble or wanted? What if he was missing? He tried to tuck his questions to the back of his mind but they nagged at him as they arrived at the field.

CHAPTER 2

When Smokey and Do What reached the baseball field, the boys were already warming up. They kept a locked trunk with their donated gloves and bats, leftover from the high school donation pile. The equipment wasn't great, but it worked. The boys gave the worn leather a bit more wear each week. They were nearly ready to head to the abandoned miner's house but figured they could get a few innings in before the sun went down. Around these parts, baseball was the best time you could have without getting into mischief.

The boys had formed their band of brothers back in the third grade. They never missed a Friday evening game.

They were led by Thomas, the eldest by two or three years. He had been born and raised in Northfork Holler and had already dropped out of school to start working in the mines. He figured there was no sense finishing school when he was just going to work as a miner anyway; why not get started early? He was large for his age, almost six feet tall, with broad shoulders and sandy brown hair that was almost always neat and groomed. He looked like a full-grown man and was treated like it in Cinder Bottom. He was the only seventeen-year-old who was allowed in the brothels without question. He was a favorite of the girls, and the other boys were envious of his privilege.

Smokey wished he could hold the same status but wasn't sure that work in the mines would be worth the increased social standing in town. Though he was considered the founder along with Do What's brother, Mike, who also worked in the mines, Thomas had moved on from the Friday night games. He spent most of his spare time outside of the mines in between the brothels of Cinder and the underground card games, gamblin' his wages away.

Two of the other members of the group were Larry and Bob—two actual brothers, just a year apart.

Larry was best characterized as the round one. He was teased about his weight but didn't mind; his mother said he was just filling out. He accepted that and used his weight to his advantage whenever possible. He couldn't sneak in the window of the miner house because he was too big so he would wait in front until someone unlocked the door. He loved Smokey's biscuits and gravy and ate nearly as much as his own father.

On one occasion, when Larry and Bob were over at the house, Smokey's dad had marveled at the boy and how much he could eat.

"Son, I know your parents feed you, but, boy, you eat like it's the last supper," he had said.

Bob, on the other hand, was slim and tall, almost frail. It was as if all of the food slipped off of his plate and landed on Larry's. His dark hair framed his thin face, and his warm brown eyes seemed to bulge slightly from his head. He wasn't much of a talker but could fix anything that had an engine or moving parts. His skills had landed him a part-time job with Mr. Williams, who repaired electric motors and machinery that broke in Cinder Bottom. Mr. Williams was hard of hearing and his eyes were bad. Since Bob wasn't much of a conversationalist, it made it a great match.

Bob had also dropped out of school to work. He didn't do hardly any of his schoolwork anyway and spent all his spare time with the brothers. The Friday evening games and hangout time were the best part of his week, though his expression would never reveal his excitement.

The last of the brotherhood was Sam Nowak, the shortest and most rebellious of the group. He was from a large Polish family, both in size and stature. Somehow, he had not reached the same height of his six-foot-tall father and siblings. Sam made up for his lack of size with his attitude and demeanor. His light brown hair and high cheekbones made him seem older than he was, though by his size you might think he was several years younger than the rest. His pale skin made his blue eyes stand out and, when he was focused, he had the look of a sniper waiting in the trees to take you down with one shot.

He was the best hitter on the team. The boys jokingly called him "No-Walk" instead of Nowak because he almost always had a run no matter how bad the pitch.

He was as smart as Smokey in his academic abilities but almost never did any schoolwork unless he was threatened to be held back. School, like life, seemed to be something of a game to Sam. Baseball was just about the only thing he took seriously, but because his grades were so bad, he never could stay on the team.

Once, when the principal had informed him that he would be cut from the team because of his grades, Sam had punctured all of the man's tires after school. This had earned him a suspension from school. For most of the boys, the Friday night ball game was just a bit of fun, but to Sam, it was the most important part of the week. Each at-bat was a matter of life and death.

Sam was already at home plate warming up when Smokey and Do What sauntered up to the dugout.

"Smoke," Larry said.

"Larry," Smokey hissed. "You boys warm up yet?"

"Naw, Sam wants to bat first, so we've just been waiting," Bob replied.

Smokey didn't say another word. He just picked up a mitt and ball and walked to the makeshift pitching mound.

The rest of the brothers slowly took the last drag of their cigarettes, grabbed a mitt, and walked to the field. They had a first and second baseman, a pitcher, and a batter. Hardly a team, but at least they all had a chance at bat. Without a catcher, every ball counted, and Sam knew it.

The boys at each base backed up to anticipate the run that was about to come their way. Smokey stood at the sandbag that served as the pitcher's mound. The brothers had taken it from a nearby drainage ditch and it did the job.

Smokey pulled the ball into his mitt as he stared intensely at an imaginary target just between Sam's knees and chest.

Smokey was a terrific pitcher and was always calm and collected. He had played ball for a while until a disrespectful coach told him he was a prima donna, and rather than slug him, Smokey had walked off the pitcher's mound and never went back. Smokey may have been the best pitcher that Northfork and Keystone had ever seen, but he refused to be disrespected. Even though the coach tried to apologize and get him back on the team, Smokey refused.

Standing at bat, Sam nodded in approval, which meant he was ready for anything that Smokey would throw at him.

Smokey wound up for the pitch and let the fastball that Sam craved go from his grip. The brothers backed up even before the pitch crossed the plate because they knew it would be a hit.

The ball sailed into the air toward left field. Larry, their best fielder, sprinted toward left field to show effort, but everyone already knew the ball would be a home run.

Sam dropped the bat, licked his lips, and almost skipped his first step before breaking into a run around the bases. The ball sailed into the bushes, and Sam jumped around third base, raising his hands in victory. This was how the game always started, with Sam's homerun. It was not even discussed; it was just how they did each game and there was no need to mess up the tradition. The boys all took turns at bat and no one kept score. Each week, the boys would brag as if each had won the world series.

After the game, walking toward the miner's house, they chatted about their prowess and how amazing they were at the game. Smokey ran back toward the field to fetch the sack of liquor he had left on the dugout bench. The boys walked past the bend and left Smokey out of sight.

Smokey snatched the bag and headed in the direction where the boys vanished. Out of the corner of his eye, he spied a shiny new car pulling up to the parking lot and slowly coming to a stop. Smokey recognized the Thunderbird, and, for a moment, he stopped in his tracks.

His heart raced, but he didn't want to attract any unnecessary attention or suspicion. He stared in the direction of the boys and didn't look back, though he knew the car belonged to the strange man he and Do What had seen speaking to the sheriff.

He was sweating but didn't change his slow, deliberate gait. He was past the dugout now and nearly to the bend in the road.

Just when he thought he was in the clear, a voice shouted, "Hey kid."

Smoke's heart sank. He hoped the man hadn't seen him in the bushes earlier. He slowly turned around and started toward the car.

The man swung the door open, got out, and then placed a felt fedora on his head.

"What's your name, son?" the man asked.

Smokey, trying to look calm, gave his Christian name. "Curtis," Smokey said in a straightforward but respectful voice.

"Well, Curtis, what are you up to?" the man demanded.

"Nothing. Just playing some ball, sir."

The man nodded disinterestedly. "Have you seen a man, about five-foot-ten, with brown hair, around here anytime recently?"

"You're describing half the people who live here in Keystone, sir," Smokey said matter-of-factly. "But no, I've seen no one unusual if that's what you mean."

Smokey wanted to ask a question but was afraid that an inquiry might give him away, so he said nothing more.

The man didn't offer any additional information. "Okay, thank you, son," he said.

He climbed back into his car and Smokey pivoted nonchalantly to leave, but he could feel the man stare at him as he made his way down the road.

Once he heard the tires rumble on the gravel parking lot, he felt confident he could look back. He watched the car drive out of sight.

Smokey was baffled. Who was the man looking for and why was he searching in Keystone? He had seen lawmen come and go, but mostly they were Feds looking to bust moonshiners to prove a point that they weren't above the law, though everyone knew they were. Heck, the sheriff got his moonshine from the same shiners as Smokey.

He touched his shirt pocket checking to see if the card with the words "Max Tucker, Agent on special assignment" was still there. He felt the edges of the card through his pocket and sprinted to catch up with the other boys.

He was out of breath once he caught up to them. He didn't want them to question his delay so before they asked, he panted, "I almost forgot the moonshine!"

The boys groaned as if to reassure him that they were grateful that he went back. They made their way toward the miner house, talking about the things that fourteen-year-old boys liked to discuss: women, boobs, and the Yankees. They started in on their usual debate over which of the boys had gotten more action with the opposite sex.

Larry was the only one on record for ever getting past third base with the girls. He had once paid for an evening at Big Ma's. Larry had been bragging about his exploits all summer. They had all been witnesses of the moment that Larry handed Big Ma five dollars and was taken by the hand to the dimly lit back room that Smokey and Do What had painted just weeks before. Larry wasn't gone very long, five minutes tops, when he emerged from the room with a gleeful smile on his face. He hadn't said a word to the other boys; he just walked right past them. He had left Big Ma's and walked home somehow different. The boys had chased him down for details, but he said nothing. Though they pestered him all the way to his house, he had not spoken a word, which was uncharacteristic of Larry, the biggest braggart of the bunch.

They all sat on his stoop when he went in talking about how much of a hero he was and that in their eyes he had grown to legendary status from that day. It was the next day that Larry told the others that he was not going back to school but rather headed to the mines to work. It was as if he had grown, changed somehow into a man, leaping over the rest of them. He was still one of the brothers, but he was never the same kid again.

When they arrived at the miner's house, they followed the usual protocol. Larry and Bob stood guard as lookouts. Sam, Do What, and Smokey went around back.

Do What squatted down to lift Smokey on his back, boosting him up to the unlocked window that they used to gain entrance to the Friday evening clubhouse.

Once inside, Smokey opened the side door to the others and whistled for Larry and Bob to join them. They had already blacked out the windows that faced the road so that the small kerosene lantern that they used for light wouldn't be seen. Larry and Bob fetched the chairs and card table they had found in the alley by the Church of God. The seats were torn and weathered, and the table was missing a leg when they found it, but with a little work, it became the perfect table to play some cards and enjoy some moonshine.

Do What pulled an old milk crate from under the sink in the kitchen, and Sam grabbed the cups they kept stashed in the cabinet. The brothers were meticulous about putting everything back in place at the end of each session; they wanted to leave no trace that they were ever there. They had heard that some other gangs used the place on Saturdays and while they didn't like the idea of sharing the secret clubhouse, they figured they all had an interest in keeping a low profile.

The evening started with a serving of the coveted moonshine, and then the card game commenced. They had used money once to play their game of cards, but a fistfight broke out between Sam and Larry, and that ended the use of money for their winnings. Instead, they used two varieties of beans as tender. They played to win but, in the end, the pot was redistributed and placed back in the old marble sack that stored the kitty. The boys laughed and drank and shared the two cigarettes that Larry had pinched from his old man.

The night seemed to slowly roll on, and the moonshine kept them warm despite the early fall air. Smokey tried to erase the events of the sheriff and the fancy new car and the stranger from his mind. He couldn't seem to let the idea of the conversation in the parking lot of the baseball field go. Smokey kept wondering what the man wanted and why the sheriff had disregarded his admonition to help. Who was this missing man? Why was he in Cinder Bottom?

The boys played and began to get annoyed at Smokey's distracted nature.

"C'mon, Smoke, what the hell are you waiting for?" Sam hissed. "Your call, show your cards."

Smokey had nothing and folded his cards.

"Man, Smokey. You're a terrible bluffer. We knew you didn't have a hand," Sam joked.

They continued to play, but Smokey was fixated on trying to figure out who the sheriff and the agent were looking for.

Smokey and his curious nature had gotten him in trouble on more than one occasion. He had witnessed a hit and run on his way home from his paper route one afternoon but had not recognized the car. He had been keen on finding out who it was because the woman that was hit was hospitalized and permanently injured. She was young but now walked with a cane like an old woman, and that didn't sit right with him.

He spent the summer searching for the person that had caused the accident. He interviewed witnesses and asked around for information about the car and the mystery assailant. In the end, he never found out who it was.

He felt like he had let that woman down, but his buddies harassed him for missing one of the Friday night gatherings and told him if he didn't show up again, he would be out. Smokey dropped it and never spoke about it again, but it still bothered him that he couldn't figure out who it was. He was the kind of boy that couldn't let go of something that he hadn't solved.

His older brothers were constantly annoyed at his questions and his persistence. For a time, his sisters thought it was cute but when it came to him questioning them about where they had been or who they were with, his incessant questioning tired them out. Even his teachers were worn out at times because he would keep asking questions about how they knew things and where did they learn it and how did they know it was true. They would respond that it was in the dang book and that should be good enough for him. But he had to know for himself why the things they said were true.

The night went on, and Smokey finally let go of some of his questions about the strange agent and the missing man. Perhaps it was the moonshine or the fun of the brothers laughing that let his mind slip from the curiosity of the sheriff's and Max Tucker's conversation.

It was nearing nine o'clock and the moonshine was gone. Sam had won most of the beans, and the boys decided to call it a night. They put away the table and chairs, stowed the cups, and blew out the lantern. The miner's house was once again back to its original state, and they all exited the door and locked it.

They walked quietly down the road toward the main part of Keystone. The house faded in the evening sky.

They didn't notice the eyes peering from the trees behind the house as they left.

The figure waited and then made his way to the window the boys used to enter and exit the house.

The boys laughed and teased each other on their way toward town before saying their goodbyes and parting ways. Smokey and Do What lived at the other end of town from the rest of the boys and walked together until they reached the holler where Do What lived.

"Well, Smoke, I guess I'll see you later," Do What said after a moment.

"See you later," Smokey replied.

There was just enough light to see, but the evening sky was darkening quickly. Smokey wanted to ask Do What what he thought about the sheriff and the agent, but he knew that Do What was more likely to be thinking about the way the light danced on the car than he did about the missing man. He appreciated Do What's simple nature and didn't want to change him. His childlike curiosity made Smokey feel at ease, like the real problems of the world were just illusions and the questions that Do What asked were the only things that mattered. Life had gotten too complex for Smokey in the last few months, and Do What's presence calmed Smokey.

Smokey could see the single light bulb that lit the main room of his home glowing in the distance. He could see the shadow of his mom standing at the sink in the kitchen, and the outline of his father smoking a cigarette, glowing with each drag, on the porch. He desperately wanted to get out of Keystone one day, but deep down he wondered if he would live out the same fate his father had, to work in the mines no matter how much he wanted to flee. His older brothers had already followed in their father's footsteps and as much as he wanted to escape, he felt that it was a hope that might never come true.

He made his way onto the porch and greeted his father, who didn't seem to have moved since he last left him.

"Evening, Pa," Smokey said.

His dad dipped his head but said nothing.

Smokey walked into the kitchen and said hi to his mother, a beautiful woman with curly brown hair that was usually pulled into a bun.

Without hesitation, she took his plate out of the oven and set it on the table. His mom was a wonderful cook. She had very little she had to work with but seemed to make gravy and biscuits seem like caviar and fine crackers. Smokey, like most people in Keystone, was satisfied by simple things: a good meal was as about as good as it gets. He always appreciated the care his mother took preparing meals, even if the ingredients were humble.

He ate his meal, took his plate up, and washed it so his mother wouldn't have to. She was busy folding laundry, and soon she'd move on to mending some of Pa's socks.

The fall air was still warm, but you could feel the temperatures beginning to change. Smokey knew that soon the chill would arrive and settle into his bones. He hoped for a few more dips into the swimming hole; it had already closed for the summer, but he and the brothers would sneak in after school and have it all to themselves.

Smokey was the youngest in his family. He was teased by his older brothers and babied by his sisters. For now, he didn't mind, but he longed for the day when they didn't see him as the baby. He wanted to be his own person, but he was always known as Charlie's younger brother or Carol's little brother. He wanted to just be Smokey, no kin to anyone.

In one of his classes, his teacher talked about New York City and the lights in the city that never sleeps. Smokey would spend hours just imagining what it must be like: fancy cars, skyscrapers, and big parties. What a wonderful adventure it would be.

He headed to his room, which he shared with his brothers, and crawled under the covers for the night. He would have to settle for his simple life in McDowell County for now and that was all right.

In the dark, his mind turned back once again to the interaction between the sheriff and the strange agent. Something about it wouldn't let him alone.

Eventually he drifted to sleep, still wondering who had gone missing.

CHAPTER
3

The next morning, Smokey arose to the smell of sausage and bacon grease. Once a month, his father would surprise them with butter, syrup, and a stack of hotcakes that he made himself. They were some of the most amazing pancakes the kids had ever tasted and it was even more special today because his father had added a few blackberries. They were a bit sour but made the meal seem so rich.

The house was full of all his family this weekend since his brother hadn't left for work yet and his sister didn't go to her babysitting job until the evening. Smokey loved his family, but he could sense that it was held together by a collective hope that someday it would all get better. Though his father had been working in the mines all his life, he worried about him. There were stories of men who were killed when a tunnel collapsed.

That's how Do What's dad broke his back. He hadn't worked for five years and didn't much leave his bed. In fact, Smokey had only seen him a few times before the accident and hadn't seen him since. Smokey was always surprised by Do What's simple reaction to his father's accident. He hadn't seemed too shaken, but Smokey knew that his family had seen some hard times in the last several years.

Do What's mother and brothers did what they could to make up for the lost income from his father, but it was never enough. Each month you could find Do What's mother at the church's food pantry getting what she could to make ends meet.

Do What never seemed to notice any problems. In fact, he would share his sandwich with Smokey on occasion. That always impressed Smokey. Smokey didn't want to let on that he knew how hard up Do What's family was, so he always took the half of sandwich and ate it with gratitude.

Do What spent most of his time at school hanging around the shop class even when he wasn't currently enrolled. He would skip other subjects like math and history to stay and work on projects. He was naturally gifted with his hands and made many cool things such as cutting boards, bird feeders, and toolboxes.

The only other class that captivated Do What was literature. He was intrigued by the writings of Whitman and Frost. Though he always flunked the class because he never turned in a single paper, he was usually the most informed and prepared student when it came to discussion. Do What knew he would end up in the mines before very long, so he figured it was a waste to try to do well in school. The primary reason he even went to school was to spend time with the brothers.

Once breakfast was over, Smokey had to take care of his chores: feed the pigs and goats, fetch water from the well to water the garden, and burn the trash from the last week. He gave the slop to the pigs and then gathered twigs and rubbish to burn in a makeshift incinerator made from an old oil barrel. He placed all the items inside, lit the fire, and covered it with a wire grate to keep the large ashes from drifting and causing a fire. He didn't mind the chores on Saturday because he didn't have to do his paper route. He would make his collections on Sunday when most people were feeling a bit more holy and generous. He always hoped for a tip here and there, but, usually, those only came during the holidays.

Smokey thought about telling his father about the sheriff and the agent, but then he would have to explain how he knew and he wasn't ready to divulge the Friday night gatherings at the abandoned miner house. Still, the interaction was keeping him puzzled and curious.

His brothers and father were headed out to Bluefield to do some business uptown. Bluefield was a bustling city in southern West Virginia. It had been born during the mining boom. There were modern buildings fifteen stories tall and streetlights and fancy bars and restaurants. Smokey seldom got to go, but when he did, he longed to stay and live a life away from the small mining town of Keystone.

When he mentioned that he couldn't wait to get out of Keystone, his mother would tell him to hush and not talk about such things. If it were up to her, he would never leave.

Being the youngest had its advantages, but it also made him feel like he wasn't seen the same way his brothers had been when they were his age. Smokey's science teacher told him that he was smart enough that if he kept up his grades, he might be able to get into college. That seemed a bit far-fetched to him, but he liked to imagine a future getting out and seeing the world and going to college.

When Smokey finished his chores, he told his mom, who was still bustling about her own work indoors, that he was headed to Geneva's in Cinder Bottom. She had asked him to replace the boards on the front porch of her storefront.

Geneva's was a restaurant turned bar in the evenings that was one of the most popular spots in Cinder Bottom. It was run by Geneva herself—a surly, stout woman who was probably once beautiful in her youth. She was a shrewd businesswoman who never had a man but took care of business on her own. She had land down in North Carolina, a farm that had been in her family for years. She would go to visit from time to time to make sure the tobacco that was raised on her property was still thriving and to check on her Uncle Sal, who was nearly eighty but still lived on the farm alone with the help of some field hands.

Geneva took a liking to Smokey and had him take care of small chores around the place, much like Big Ma did. She let him bring Do What along for help, though he was more interested in spending time with Smokey than doing any work.

Smokey and Do What worked for a few hours, with Do What chattering all the while. Once they had finished, they went beneath the porch to pick up all of the fallen nails; they figured they could use them to repair the miner house. The porch was raised, and there was enough room to get down on their hands and knees to gather the nails in a small sack.

Smokey and Do What were out of sight beneath the porch when they heard the voice of the stranger from the other day. Smokey shushed Do What so he could hear what he was talking to Geneva about.

"Good afternoon, ma'am," the agent said. "Any sighting as of this morning?"

Through the boards, Smokey could tell the man was holding a picture. He moved back and forth under the porch to try to catch a glimpse between the boards. He held his finger up to his lips in anticipation of the inevitable questions Do What was preparing to ask.

"Look, mister. I told you I ain't seen that man. I got work to do, so if you don't mind, I need to go," Geneva retorted.

The man didn't seem convinced.

"Mind if I take a look around?" He made his way inside without waiting for her response. "I won't be but a moment," the agent said.

Geneva didn't argue with him but shouted instead, "Try the sweet potato pie if you're gonna stay around." She stomped off the porch, got into her truck, and then bounced down the road.

Smokey turned to Do What. "Come on, let's go."

They crawled out from under the porch and made their way to the window of Geneva's to see what the man was up to. He stood next to a booth with a few men. He said something to them, and the men shook their heads in response to his questioning.

Who is this man looking for? Smokey wondered. *And why is he so persistent?* Men who came to Cinder Bottom didn't want to be found, and no one was ever going to tell the agent who he was even if they knew. But Smokey wondered why he hadn't seen this mystery man himself. Smokey made it his business to watch the coming and goings-on of Cinder Bottom.

The man turned to look out the window, and the boys ducked, hoping that they weren't seen. They didn't wait to find out and ran without looking back. The man stepped out onto the porch to light a cigarette just as they disappeared around the corner.

Smokey knew he needed more answers, and he knew just the place to start: the sheriff. Maybe the sheriff knew more than he had let on. Smokey knew he would have to be cautious with his questions because he didn't want to raise the sheriff's suspicion.

He and Do What headed to the small coffee shop down the road where Sheriff Donnie often could be found shooting the breeze and drinking his fair share of coffee. They only had sixty-seven cents between them, which was enough for a hot chocolate and a donut to share.

They sat close to the sheriff, who was finishing telling Maxine, the youthful waitress behind the counter, one of his tales of valor. Just behind the corner stool stood a man that Smokey did not recognize. He and Do What chose to sit close to the sheriff to see if they could glean some details about the agent or the missing man.

As they settled into their seats, they heard the sheriff sigh in response to something Maxine had said.

"Maxine, they're all the same. They come into town, acting like they own the place, these Feds. They think they can just pressure the law in McDowell County, but they have another thing coming to them," the sheriff said.

"Well, Donnie, I'm sure you handled it," Maxine responded.

"Hell right, I did. It won't be long before he leaves like the last one," he said.

Smokey leaned in closer toward the sheriff, waving at him. The sheriff barely noticed him and continued to gloat about his other acts of heroism.

Maxine winked at Smokey. She liked him and thought he was cute for a boy his age. If he was ten years older, she would have chased after him.

Smokey and Do What ordered their hot chocolate and shared a plain donut as they waited for more information.

"All I know, Maxine," the sheriff continued as she refilled his coffee cup, "is that agent better not get in my way. There is too much at stake for Cinder Bottom, and anything that could lead to trouble here for us needs to be squashed."

Maxine nodded but didn't respond. She glanced at the man at the end of the counter, who stared intently at his plate and ate quickly without looking up, sipping coffee between each bite.

"Hey, Sheriff Donnie," Smokey said, tired of not being noticed.

The sheriff said hi but didn't skip a beat going on about his police accomplishments.

"So, you looking for someone?" Smokey asked, interrupting the sheriff. Donnie looked quickly at Smokey and gave him a forceful glance.

"Who told you I was looking for anyone?" he said.

"Oh, no one," Smokey said, trying to play off like he knew less than he did. "I thought I heard you say you might have been looking for someone."

"Don't you worry, Smokey. There ain't nobody to be looking for. You gotta be missing in order to be found. Otherwise, you're just minding your business," said the sheriff. "And we all know how to mind our business in Cinder Bottom, now don't we, Smokey?"

The sheriff looked annoyed that Smokey had interrupted his flirting with Maxine. He had been trying to get her to go out on a date with him for months, without any success.

Smokey knew he should drop it before he really irritated the sheriff, but he wasn't ready to let it go.

He glanced down the end of the bar looking for the man at the corner stool, but he was gone. He hadn't noticed him leave. His coffee cup was still full of hot coffee and his food was half-eaten. Where had he gone, and who was he? It must not have been the man the agent was looking for or he would have been more obvious.

It was strange, though, that a man was in Cinder Bottom that Smokey didn't recognize. He made his way around the entire area every day for his paper route, and he usually noticed even the smallest change in inhabitants. Though it was possible that a stranger was just passing through, it still made him question who the man was and why he was in such a hurry to leave. Perhaps it was just a coincidence, but Smokey was still suspicious.

Do What seemed oblivious to anything besides slowly dunking the donut in his hot chocolate.

"Man, this is good, Smokey," Do What said, somewhat in an altered state of bliss.

Sometimes Do What would hyperfocus on a task or a moment, and everything else seemed to slip by him. Smokey was used to it but was always puzzled by how Do What could so easily tune out everything. It served Do What well, though. At home, if he didn't tune out what was going on, he might get caught up in the bickering between his parents who were always trying to make ends meet ever since his father's accident. It wasn't that Do What didn't care; it was that he genuinely didn't seem to notice.

The sheriff, having struck out once again with the pretty waitress, grabbed his hat and told Maxine to consider his proposal about a date the following week. She raised the towel that she was wiping the counter with but didn't acknowledge him.

Hoping that he might get a little more information from Maxine, Smokey called her over.

"Maxine, who was the sheriff looking for? He seemed bothered," Smokey said.

"He's all bent out of shape by some federal agent who was looking for a man from D.C. that has been missing for a few weeks. He was supposedly here but no one has seen him and the sheriff seems to think the agent is trying to show that he isn't doing a good job of keeping the law in Cinder Bottom," Maxine said.

"Oh, who is the man?" Smokey asked.

"I don't know, but I think he's someone important in Washington because that agent was in here the other day asking me questions and let on that it was some bigwig official."

Smokey's curiosity started to rise. Why would they be looking for a bigwig in Cinder Bottom if there was no evidence he was here? Where was he, and where could he be hiding if he was here?

"Thank you, Maxine, for the donut and chocolate," Smokey said, placing his sixty-seven cents on the counter. She picked up a dime and pushed the remaining coins toward him.

"The dime is for the donut. The hot chocolate is on me, boys," Maxine said as she winked and went across the restaurant to help others.

Smokey shouted to her, "Thanks, Maxine!"

She turned and winked and went on to take orders from the guests.

Smokey turned to Do What, who was smiling with a joyful grin from the donut.

"Did you see that man at the end of the counter? He sure left in a hurry," Smokey said. "He didn't even finish his coffee or food."

"Why don't you check his wallet, Smoke? He left his jacket on the chair," Do What said as he used his spoon to get the last bit of whipped cream from his cup.

Smokey stared. How had he noticed the man leave his jacket when Smokey hadn't even seen the man leave? Do What, always full of surprises, was right; the jacket hung on the back of the bar chair.

Smokey calmly walked past the jacket at the seat, brushing it as he passed, and was able to snag the wallet inside. He motioned for Do What to join him in the phone booth near the restrooms. Smokey wasn't proud of it, but he was good at swiping wallets and had on occasion taken a few dollars from visitors. He even placed the billfolds back in their pockets without them even noticing. He was sure his grandmother would tell him that pulling stunts like that would earn him a seat in hell.

Once inside the phone booth, Smokey slipped an ID card out of the wallet. The card read, "Peter Rose, 28, 5'10", brown hair, lives in Bethesda, Maryland." Inside the wallet, they found some cash, a few receipts (one from the local boarding house), and a small stack of business cards that read, "Peter Rose, Aide to Congressman Roger Riley."

Smokey wondered if this could be who the agent and the sheriff were looking for. This would explain why the agent was so secretive. If a congressman was in Cinder Bottom, that meant he was probably doing what most men who came from the northeast did: stay invisible, enjoy the liquor and the women, and then leave.

At that moment there was a pounding on the door of the phone booth. Both boys jumped and

nearly squealed. Earl, the town mechanic, was looking in annoyed.

"Come on, boys. I gotta make a call!" Earl yelled.

Smokey quickly hid the wallet behind his back
and exited the phone booth.

As they made their way toward the door, they
saw the man, Peter Rose, asking Maxine a question.
She pointed to the chair where he had sat earlier and
where the jacket still hung. Smokey and Do What had
just brushed past it and returned the wallet almost
without effort.

They hurried past the man out the front door.
Smokey couldn't help but notice the deep bags and
dark circles under his eyes. The man was young but
seemed to be carrying a heavy burden. They glanced
back to see the man check his pocket for his billfold.
He grabbed his coat and headed toward the door after
Smokey and Do What.

The boys quickly went around the building and
watched to see where the man went. He flung the
jacket over his shoulder and walked across the street
toward the boarding house. Smokey and Do What
waited for Peter Rose to be far enough away that they
wouldn't be noticed and headed in his direction.

The man walked into the office of the boarding house, and Smokey and Do What trailed behind,
trying not to draw attention to themselves.

The boarding house was run by Lorenzo, an Italian
man whose family had moved to West Virginia to

work in the coal camp years before. He had inherited the boarding house from his grandfather Alessandro. It was clean, convenient, and not terribly glamorous, but it did the job if you wanted a decent place to stay.

Lorenzo didn't allow any drinking, gambling, or call girls; you had to go to Geneva's or Big Ma's place for those sort of things. Lorenzo wanted to cater to what he called good folk.

The doors to the boarding house faced the street, and it was obvious from the office window when people came and went. If someone wanted to sneak away, they would have to do it in the middle of the night when the office was empty.

The boys watched Peter Rose enter Room 8, looking both ways and behind him before entering. He quickly closed the door behind him. He drew the curtains, and then stillness remained.

The boys made their way to the front desk to see Lorenzo. They had often done odd jobs for him to earn a little extra cash. It wouldn't seem strange for them to stop by to ask about work.

Lorenzo was a round man with jet black hair and a thick mustache. He wore the same outfit every day: simple khaki slacks and black button-down short-sleeve shirt. It was his uniform; the idea of having to choose what he would wear seemed like a waste of time to him.

When the boys entered the office, Lorenzo was smoking a cigarette, his one vice, and reading the

Bluefield Daily Telegraph. He liked to be caught up with what was going on in the big city and would often talk about how he was gonna sell his place and move up to Bluefield. He wished he could have a reputable establishment instead of being stuck in Cinder Bottom like his father. Lorenzo had been talking about leaving as long as Smokey could remember.

The office was dated but warmly decorated; it was largely the same as when Lorenzo's mother had first designed it nearly forty years before. It had a sense of Italian charm with photos of Sofia Loren and the Amalfi coast. Lorenzo's parents had died fifteen years ago, the year before Smokey was born. Lorenzo had never married. Instead, he had dedicated himself to running the boarding house. Part of him felt like if he left to see the world or find a bride that part of his parents memory would fade as well.

The boys opened the door, making a small bell jingle over their heads. Lorenzo peeked over his paper to greet the boys. He had a fondness for them and often gave them work even if he didn't really need it because he liked the occasional company.

"Hi, boys, what brings you in? So good to see you," Lorenzo chirped. He put the paper down and rose to his feet to greet them.

"Hi, Signore Lorenzo," Smokey said, and Do What tipped his ball cap. Though he was a silent partner most of the time, Do What knew how to treat adults with respect, unlike the rest of the brothers. Smokey rarely did these sorts of things with Sam, Larry, or Bob; they were often just too shortsighted to be polite.

"What are you boys up to today?" Lorenzo asked.

"Nothing much Signore Lorenzo. What's new and exciting around here today?" Smokey said, knowing that Lorenzo often liked to discuss the news from the paper and the happenings outside of Cinder Bottom. He figured he might get some information from him about his suspicious guest Peter Rose.

Smokey positioned himself so he could speak to Lorenzo and still have a clear line of sight out the window to Room 8, in case Peter left.

Do What was engrossed in eating his fill from a bowl of peanuts left out for guests. Lorenzo didn't mind. In fact, he set them out for the boys because they were often the only ones who ate them.

The ornate Italian-style lounge area made Smokey feel as if he was back in time in some small village in Italy. He would often imagine what it would be like to see the world and all the amazing countries, cultures, and food. He longed to explore and loved to hear Lorenzo speak of his family's villas in Umbria, just south of Tuscany.

"Smokey, it's the same here. Not much is different. But I hear up in Bluefield they have a new bowling alley that is supposed to be amazing! Lanes light up, a nice restaurant inside, said to be one of the best on the east coast," Lorenzo said with confidence.

Bowling was the one sport that Smokey didn't play, mainly because there was no bowling alley in McDowell County. Smokey was good at any sport with a ball and figured if he ever had the chance, he would try bowling and see what the hype was all about.

"So, no new interesting people visiting Cinder Bottom these days?" Smokey asked. He hoped for a bit more information about Mr. Rose and would let Lorenzo lead with anything he had.

"Well, a few new guests, some from far away and others just regulars," he said.

Smokey was now ready to dive in for more.

"How far away?" Smokey said.

"Washington, D.C., some government-type people. Not sure why they are here, but they seem to be looking for someone," Lorenzo said.

"People? So more than one visitor from D.C.?" Smokey asked.

"Yeah, two fellas. They don't seem to be together though. One is staying here and the other is in Bluefield. The guest who's staying here, he's a quiet, nervous fella. Nice enough though. He's been here a few days already. Supposed to check out tomorrow," Lorenzo said.

He felt like maybe he had said too much to the boys, but he was longing for company and conversation and figured that the boys would be the easiest to chat with. Why would they care who came and went?

He continued to tell the boys about the man. What car he drove, how much ice he requested, his need for multiple towels, and his leaving in the middle of the night. While some might find all these details to be trivial in nature, they were exactly the kind of particulars that Lorenzo kept track of on all his patrons. He had a strong memory and usually didn't leave out many details.

He finished by telling the boys how he saw the man with someone else one night, a man he didn't recognize. When Lorenzo had exhausted his information about the man and all the other town gossip, he told the boys he had to run out to check a room. He asked them to mind the office and to tell anyone who came that he would be right back.

When Smokey was certain that the coast was clear and Lorenzo was gone, he went behind the front desk and began to look at the guest ledger, looking for Room 8. He was halfway down the second page when the door opened and the bell sounded.

In walked Peter Rose.

The startled look on Smokey's face changed quickly from alarmed to helpful.

Putting on a smile, Smokey said, "Good morning, sir, how may I help you?" as if he had perfectly rehearsed it.

The man made his way reluctantly to the front desk and fidgeted with his hat in his hands. He wore a button-down shirt and slacks, the bags under his eyes were noticeable, and he seemed to be hunching over a bit as if timid. He had sneakers on, which struck Smokey as odd since he was wearing trousers and a dress shirt.

"Is Mr. Lorenzo here?" the man asked.

"He stepped out, but is there something I can help you with?' Smokey asked with confidence.

"Well, can you tell Mr. Lorenzo when he returns that I would like to have some extra towels delivered to my room?" said Mr. Rose.

"You bet I will, sir. What's your name and room number?" Smokey asked, taking a pencil and paper from the drawer.

"My name is Mr. Brown. I'm in Room 8," Peter said in a strong Yankee accent. He was clearly from somewhere way up north. Obviously not from around these parts.

"And a first name, sir?" Smokey asked, trying to figure out his real name.

"Arnold, Arnold Brown," Peter said. "Thank you, kindly." He walked out.

Smokey was now curious. Was Peter's name really Arnold Brown? Why would he lie about his name? Smokey looked up the guest register, and he was registered as Arnold Brown, Room 8. Smokey wrote out the note to notify Lorenzo of the request and taped it to his desk.

"Let's go," Smokey said to Do What. "We need to go see someone."

Smokey and Do What left quickly, not waiting for Lorenzo to return. Smokey had a hunch, and he needed to check it out. Do What, who was always amicable, followed closely behind without questioning him.

Smokey knew where he had to go to get more information: Raymond's grocery store. He always went there when he needed some information that was hard to come by. His friend Raymond, the owner of the store, always knew what was going on in Bluefield. The city was made famous by the discovery of the richest deposit of coal in the world. At its height, it was one of America's fastest-growing cities, behind New York City and Chicago.

Bluefield's high elevation and proximity to one of the richest coal seams in the world, the Pocahontas Coal Field, positioned it to be the railroad headquarters in the region. The coal mined from the outlying areas around Cinder Bottom was loaded onto train cars. From Bluefield, the trains moved millions of tons of coal to be loaded onto ships in Hampton Roads. Bluefield was considered such an important location during WWII that the city was listed on Hitler's map of strategic targets.

Bramwell, an area just outside of Bluefield, was said to be the millionaire capital of America with more millionaires per capita than anywhere else in the country. Bluefield was one of the largest cities in the state and drew wealthy and influential people from around the northeast. Smokey suspected that the answers to the questions he was seeking lay in the city, not in Cinder Bottom.

It was hard to truly disappear in a small town like Cinder Bottom. If there was going to be a man missing, it would be in a larger city. In Bluefield, there were simply too many people to keep track of all of them. Smokey needed to know what was going on outside of Cinder if he was going to get to the bottom of things about the missing man.

When he got to Raymond's grocery store, he went around back to look for Raymond. He found him in his usual spot, perched up on some sacks of flour used as pillows with the *Bluefield Daily Telegraph* draped across his body.

"Raymond," Smoke said loud enough to be heard but not loud enough to frighten him. He was known to hide a pistol under his shirt. Smokey didn't want to be a casualty from waking him.

Raymond jerked awake and stared down at the end of his glasses.

"Oh, it's you, Smoke. You damn near gave me a heart attack," he said. He sat upright and pulled the paper from off his chest. "What are you boys up to?"

"Nothing, just here to visit you," Smokey said.

Do What moved closer now that Raymond was awake and there was less of a chance of his pistol going off.

Raymond was the owner of the corner store. It was the only black-owned grocery in Cinder Bottom— and maybe the whole state for that matter. It wasn't a colored-only store either; anyone was allowed. No special entrances for black folks, and no special privilege for being white. It had been this way for as long as Smokey could remember, but he realized from the times he visited his Aunt Annie in North Carolina that segregation was a real thing and that the rules outside didn't apply to Cinder Bottom in many ways.

Ray had been running the store for nearly twenty-nine years and he knew more about what happened between Cinder Bottom and Bluefield than anyone else in town. He made several trips a week to Bluefield, and even Bramwell on occasion, to get more supplies. One of the treats for his journey would be his copy of the *Bluefield Daily Telegraph*. Unlike the local paper that Smokey delivered on his paper route, this paper was about the events in the big city and beyond. If there was going to be news about a prominent figure in D.C. that had gone missing, it would be reported in the *Daily Telegraph*.

Smokey noticed that the paper that Ray was reading was from today.

"Are you finished with your paper, Ray?" Smokey asked.

Ray shrugged and handed it to Smokey. He liked that a boy his age cared about what was going on in the world. He and Smokey would often talk about the latest news.

"You can have it. I'm finished," Ray said. He stood up and brushed a few crumbs off his shirt. Ray was a large black man, with hands that would swallow up yours if he gave you a handshake, though he was never too forceful with his grip.

"Thanks, Ray!" Smokey quickly scanned the front page for any story that might be a clue to uncovering the mystery of the missing man.

Do What came to his side and placed his finger in the bottom right column. The headline read, "Junior Congressman Roger Riley Gone AWOL?"

"Do you think this is him?" Do What asked.

Smokey turned the page and looked for the continuation of the article. There at the bottom of page 6 was "Roger Riley, Junior Congressman." The article explained that Congressman Riley had not been seen on the Hill or at his home district in almost three weeks. Though there was evidence, according to the article, that he was in contact with some officials in Washington. It was unclear why he hadn't been seen, but some speculated that it was a deliberate attempt to resist the call for his party to stand together in protest of Brown vs. The Board of Education case, which had ended segregation in public schools. If he refused to show up to cast his support, he would be seen as a traitor. No further information about his whereabouts was known at this time.

Smokey stared at Do What and realized that Ray was still on the porch moving some sacks of potatoes from his truck.

"Hey, Ray," Smokey called out to him. "Anything interesting going on in Bluefield?"

"I hear lots of interesting things when I go to Bluefield. So much is happening in the world. I listen to the radio on the way in too and get the big city stations when I get there."

Smokey wasn't sure how to bring up the congressman without arousing suspicions in Ray. He knew that Ray prided himself on knowing every detail about the latest headlines so that he could talk to his suppliers in Bluefield without being judged as ignorant or thought of as a second-class citizen, the way most other black folks felt when they left Cinder Bottom.

In the safety and security of Cinder Bottom, Ray was respected by both whites and blacks, and he seldom had to face the prejudices that he had grown up with in Baltimore as a kid. His parents had come to this area to be sharecroppers during the depression and eventually made their way to Cinder Bottom by accident. Their truck broke down, the same one that Ray still drove. His father became a bootlegger and worked in the mines. With the small amount of money that his father left behind, Ray started the corner store.

He enjoyed a peaceful existence and was the man you went to when you needed anything. If you needed to know if your daughter was sneaking around, Ray would know. If you wanted to know who helped themselves to the offering tray at the local Church of God during midweek services, Ray knew. He seemed to know all, but he was tight-lipped, and rather than pay Raymond for information, people paid Ray to keep quiet. He knew more than most. He could keep things quiet and would guard any of his secrets with his life, and everyone knew it.

The sheriff must have come to him and asked if he knew of any strange men who were in town. Smokey thought that there was a good chance Ray either knew exactly where the congressman was or he knew someone who knew where he was. Getting him to say what he knew would be a different story, though.

Pretending to care less than he was putting on, Smokey looked up from behind the front page and asked, "Hey Ray, did you read about the missing congressman?"

Ray raised an eyebrow and then said quickly, "I think I did read about that; he's been missing for a few weeks." He moved quickly to get the next sack of potatoes and Do What followed to help.

Do What heaved a sack up to the porch and was already out of breath. Do What was athletic but not in top physical condition.

Ray lifted up two sacks and effortlessly placed them onto the porch before grabbing Do What's sack and piling it on top of the others. He patted Do What on the back, thanking him for his effort.

"It sure seems strange that he would just disappear for no reason, especially being the new guy," Smokey said.

Ray turned to him, looking puzzled. "Well, I guess he really doesn't want to support the Southern Manifesto," Ray said.

Smokey could tell that Ray was not giving up any more information about the congressman, even if he knew.

"What's that?" Smokey asked.

"The Southern Manifesto is the South's resistance to oppose public school integration," Ray said.

He knew that Smokey understood because they discussed the case at length when the case was at the supreme court. Why anyone would care if blacks and whites went to school together was beyond Smokey, but he understood the power of racism and how it impacted many people. Big Ma talked about it often to Smokey, as well. Something about Smokey's interest made it easy for adults to treat him as an equal when it came to politics and current events.

The reason he was so intrigued by the local paper route that he had was that he received a free paper. His father enjoyed it too, but he wasn't much for talking about what he read—he just looked at the sports page and nothing more.

Big Ma and Ray would sit and discuss the things that they had read in the evenings. They didn't want people to think they thought themselves as better than anyone else, so they had these conversations out of earshot. They wanted to stay informed, and they never missed a chance to discuss what Ray discovered during his trips to Bluefield. Big Ma's place would be Smokey's next stop to see what she might know.

Ray seemed content enough that Smokey was just being curious, so he continued to give his opinion on the missing congressman.

"Maybe this might be a good thing if a congressman from the South refuses to side with the others. However, it might make for a short career for a junior congressman," Ray said.

Smokey thanked him for the paper and his perspective. Do What tipped his baseball cap, and with that, they left.

He was still puzzled by what Ray said about the congressman. What did he mean it might be a short career? He didn't want to get sidetracked by that so he decided to mentally set that aside and head over to Big Ma's.

Once the boys were off the porch and out of earshot, they started to talk about what they had learned. Could the agent be looking for the congressman in Cinder Bottom? If he was hiding there, why? What made this a convenient place to hide? Was it because the reputation that nothing leaves Cinder Bottom makes it a prime place to hide?

Something didn't seem to add up for Smokey, and he couldn't figure out what the congressman had to gain by hiding. Why not just oppose the manifesto? Why hide?

Smokey did most of the talking, and Do What just listened, as usual. He never interrupted Smokey when he was on a roll.

CHAPTER
4

On their way to Big Ma's, they discussed what they were going to do for lunch. They were starving, and the donut and hot chocolate were long gone. They thought about waiting to have barbecue at Big Ma's in the evening, but their stomachs ached, and they couldn't wait that long.

They knew that Geneva had a lunch plate that was a dollar, but their remaining fifty-seven cents wouldn't cover it. They opted to get a plate of biscuits and gravy that was only fifty cents and shared a pop for a nickel, leaving them with two cents to spare.

Do What and Smokey were used to sharing. They shared most things, like liquor and cigarettes, but they drew lines at sharing girls. It was code that you didn't get with your buddy's girl even if she wanted to. Smokey had a way of attracting older women, even women that were married, without even trying.

Larry was often the one the brothers admired for his sexual prowess, but Smokey was a close second, and the boys knew better than to let their girls talk with him or they might dump them for him. It wasn't something he said or did, it was just the way he carried himself. It was like he was already a grown man because he was able to speak intelligently to just about anyone, and that made some of the men in town hate Smokey. They would scowl at him when their girls or wives waved to him when he passed by or when he brought their papers to the door during his paper route. Smokey knew they were flirting with him, but he couldn't resist the attention; what fourteen-year-old boy could?

He was handsome, with a wavy tuft of hair greased perfectly. He looked good in a T-shirt and jeans and even more so when he had a pair of nice pants and a button-down shirt, probably borrowed from his older brother Vince who was married and lived up the road. He didn't try to attract women and girls; it was his natural charm that did that. Smokey didn't mind and he used it to his advantage whenever necessary.

It was his charm that made Big Ma like him. She wasn't taken in by it like the others. She just appreciated that he had it and knew how to use it. She liked the way he treated her girls and often did things for them, even if Big Ma didn't ask him to. He would bring them flowers or get the comics from the Telegraph that Ray gave him on Sundays because he knew they liked them. He didn't try to make any moves on the girls, which is why Big Ma trusted him. He knew his place and not to cross the line with her.

Big Ma was not someone to be messed with. She didn't hold a grudge but she never forgot. She didn't need to be forgiving because she never gave anyone the benefit of the doubt. She knew that if you give anyone the benefit of the doubt, that you could open up yourself to be hurt, and Big Ma vowed never to be hurt by anyone again. Not since her grandpa basically offered her up to a church deacon in exchange for a favor when she was a twelve-year-old girl living in Tennessee.

She managed to escape from the deacon's room when he attempted to make sexual advances on her. She literally ran out of town making it as far as she could on foot. When she had been found wandering the back roads of North Carolina by Harold Baker, hitching a ride to Cinder Bottom was the opportunity she had to get herself even further away. She knew she would never go back home.

She must have walked for two days with no food or water before she was found nearly half-starved with no shoes, bleeding from the long walk. Harold was driving a pickup load of supplies to Cinder Bottom and offered her a ride if she sat in the back. He didn't want to be seen driving with a colored girl in his pickup. She didn't mind because he gave her some coffee and a piece of his sandwich, which she devoured the moment she touched it. The coffee, too, went down in an instant. She never liked coffee, but at that moment it was the best thing she ever had. She was tired and weary and fell asleep in the bed of the truck, no idea where she was headed and not really caring as long as it was as far away from Tennessee as she could get.

When they arrived in Cinder Bottom, Big Ma was dropped off in front of the house she would eventually own. At that time, it was run by a woman named Marge.

There were no colored-owned whore houses at that time but young colored girls were in big demand, so Marge took Ma in and gave her a place to sleep and food in exchange for her tending the bar and cleaning the rooms after the girls finished with their men for the night. Ma would wash the sheets in a large tub out back and hang them to dry during the day. She didn't mind the work and figured it was better than where she came from.

Though many men asked about her, Marge refused to let her be with men. She was too young, and Marge wanted to let her come of age. She knew what she had been through and didn't want to push her too soon because she was afraid she might run.

Ma was a lovely young girl—her hair and her skin were beautiful until she started puberty. That's when the acne started to scar her face. It became so severe that she had to soak compresses to keep the sores from oozing and bursting. Her beauty remained, but the scars on her face kept her from being called on by men when she did come of age.

Marge let her stay on to tend to the cleaning and to continue caring for the women. She learned to cook and her timid demeanor started to change as she grew more and more tired of the mean names that the men would call her: crater face, pockmark, or worse. Her once bright, hopeful manner started to fade and the hard, tough exterior replaced it.

She grew as a woman and her figure filled out as she grew tall, almost as tall as some of the men. She learned not to take lip from anyone.

One night, when a man tried to take advantage of her, she grabbed a knife from the counter and stabbed him in the arm. He was so angry that he slapped her halfway across the room and was probably going to kill her when Marge stepped in and aimed a gun at him right in the crotch. She told him to leave and never come back. He stood there bleeding and heaving and started to try to take the gun from her, and she shot him, shooting off his penis. He rolled on the floor in agony and nearly died right there.

Marge was arrested, and the man was rushed to Bluefield Sanitarium but died on the operating table. Marge was eventually released but soon after disappeared and never returned. No one knew if she was hunted down by the man's kin or if she just decided enough was enough.

The girls of the house weren't sure what to do when she didn't return, but Big Ma just kept the place running, and the doors had been open ever since.

The house slowly became the most popular house in Cinder Bottom. Both white and black men loved Big Ma's house. Big Ma kept the same rifle behind the bar that Marge used to shoot the man. Both Marge and Big Ma were legendary. Only one or two people were still around who remembered that night, but the story was regularly told and retold by patrons of Big Ma's. Knowing that Big Ma trusted Smokey was a big deal, and Smokey knew it.

When the boys arrived at Big Ma's, the girls were on the porch drinking some sweet tea and gossiping. They were beautiful women with long flowing silk dresses, big smiles, and figures that stopped anyone in their tracks. Smokey had forgotten to get the comics from the paper, but he figured he would come back the next day since the Sunday comics were the best and Ray would always save them for him.

Sharon, the eldest girl, was getting the grill ready for their afternoon barbecue. They often sat outside when the weather was good and sang popular songs on the radio. It was as if they were all singers in another life. Big Ma said it was because the girls all grew up in the church that they could sing so well. Smokey didn't really understand why because his grandmother sang in the church but sounded like a cat being skinned. She would call it a joyful noise unto the Lord, but to Smokey it was just noise and he wasn't certain why the Lord needed such a racket since he could hardly stand it.

The girls were usually between sixteen and twenty-two. Once they reached a certain age and stopped being requested by the gentlemen callers, they would run off with one of their johns. Big Ma didn't try to stop them. She knew what it was like to be kept and didn't want the girls to feel that way.

A lot of young girls, mostly runaways, found their way to Big Ma's. She always offered to help. If they were fit to be with the men, she gave them the opportunity to work. If they weren't to work in the house, she gave them some money and sent them to work in one of the restaurants or to Bluefield where they might be better suited. She didn't want a girl to go hungry or be mistreated, and she also knew that some of these girls had no place to go.

Big Ma had no family besides these girls, and she treated them that way whether they stayed a week or a few years. Often, some of the women would come back to visit. They had jobs or a family now, and they held a special place in their hearts for Big Ma. She was both the villain and the savior for these girls. The women had sold their bodies for the pleasure of men, but in the end many of them found themselves better off than they had been before Big Ma found them.

Big Ma would never leave Cinder Bottom; there was nothing out there for her. She knew who she was and didn't mind the life she had built. The isolation and the microcosm that she lived in was enough, and her world evolved around her place in it.

Big Ma was away doing some errands about town for the afternoon. She didn't drive, so she had Raymond drive her to town on occasion. That suited her, being chauffeured around. She would dress in flowing gowns and big hats and fur coats, which made her stand out wherever she went. Men in Bluefield gave a gentle nod to pay respects when she passed by, but otherwise didn't give any impression that they knew who she was. They didn't want to attract attention to their acquaintance with the madam of the colored brothel in Cinder Bottom.

She would stop in at the counter at Kresge's to have a donut and an ice-cold Coca Cola. She ignored the sign that said "whites only" and expected service anyway. Every once in a while, a new waitress would ask her to leave, not understanding Big Ma's notoriety in the community of Cinder and in the entire region. Big Ma would ignore her and motion for one of the other girls behind the counter to bring her the usual, and without hesitation the other waitresses did. White women would scoff at her boldness, and some would get up and leave. That didn't bother Big Ma any, she just kept on eating her donut and drinking her Coke until she was ready to leave.

It was always a spectacle to watch Big Ma enter any establishment. She didn't much care for the townspeople in their natural habitat, with their judging eyes and hushed whispers about who she was. In Cinder Bottom, everyone, even those city folks that visited the town, knew that judgment didn't belong there because everyone knew why you were there, and to judge others was to judge yourself.

Big Ma tolerated her visits to the bank and to shop in Bluefield, but she preferred Cinder Bottom and quickly returned the moment her errands were done.

Big Ma never attended school after the fifth grade but knew more about the world than most in Cinder Bottom because she was a voracious reader. She would check out library books and read the local and national papers and discuss the biggest issues at hand with Ray, who also loved to read.

It was always a wonder why Big Ma and Ray never got together since they were both unmarried. They both seemed content to have their own lives and stay single, though there was an undeniable energy between them. Smokey tried to ask Ray once why he was still single and was told that he better keep his mind in the newspaper and out of anyone else's business. That was a cardinal rule around Cinder Bottom, and to violate that could mean trouble for you.

The boys' mouths started to salivate when they rounded the back of Big Ma's house, smelling the smoke pouring from the fire pit. The smell reminded them of the amazing food that was coming: ribs, corn on the cob, collard greens, and cornbread.

Big Ma always put on a feast on Saturday for her girls. The smell filled the bottom and people all around would come to visit Ma and have a glass of sweet tea. It was like a family reunion in Cinder Bottom. They would reminisce about the old days, listen to the radio, and sing songs. Everyone brought a side dish to contribute: bread or pop or a helping of mashed potatoes.

It was odd for Smokey to see such a joyful gathering of people who weren't kin. It was as if they didn't have a care in the world, just being alive was enough. Smokey always felt strange when he watched Big Ma. All he could think of was getting himself out of Cinder Bottom while Big Ma could think of nowhere else she wanted to be.

The food was getting ready to be served, and Do What and Smokey were useful, bringing out folding chairs for the older folk, bringing out the trash can to collect rubbish, and gathering more wood for the fire.

Smokey and Do What were always welcome around Big Ma's. They helped because they wanted to. They didn't expect to be fed, but always appreciated the plates of food that Big Ma would give them.

Big Ma pulled up just as the food was ready, her timing perfect as usual. Big Ma was never late or not where she wanted to be. When Smokey had once asked her how come she was always at the right place at the right time, she'd said, "Baby, that's because the good Lord knows where I need to be and when I need to be there."

The gathered guests raised their glasses full of sweet tea when she arrived and a few even clapped. This was the reception she loved and not the kind she would get in Bluefield or anywhere else. This is why she never wanted to leave the Bottom; her chosen family was here and nothing in her mind could be better. Smokey, though his family was there, could think of a dozen places he'd rather be than stuck in Cinder Bottom.

They all enjoyed their meal and the warmth of the fire where fun stories and dramatic tales would be shared. Do What felt at home there as much as Smokey, mainly because he was accustomed to accepting things as they were. His house was not a place to call home. His parents fought often since his father's accident, and his brother was frequently drunk and almost never home.

Do What, like Big Ma, had no desire to leave the Bottom. This puzzled Smokey since Do What seemed to have a miserable home life.

Do What knew that he would work in the mines one day and fantasized about becoming a patron at Big Ma's. He often stared a little too long at the girls, admiring their beauty, long legs, and sense of allure. He hoped that one day he could whisk one of them away as his wife and live happily ever after, but that was more of a dream than a reality. Though it was accepted to lay with a girl at Big Ma's, it was another thing for a white man and a black woman to carry on in a relationship. Do What knew that—everyone did— but that didn't keep him from dreaming about it.

He told Smokey about his fantasies but not the other brothers. Do What longed to be part of a family like the one Big Ma had built. They wouldn't understand. It angered Do What when they would say things like, "Why would you want to be with a whore?" Do What would never talk like that and he tackled Sam and pounded his face, giving him a black eye, for saying such a thing.

Do What was mostly a passive guy, but that is where he drew the line. It was almost as if he became possessed when Sam said those words. Smokey might occasionally say that word if Do What wasn't around, but then he did feel bad about it. It was just so common that it would slip his mind, even if he didn't mean any harm.

There were so many pretty girls who wanted to get with Do What, but he always refused. It was as if he was saving himself for someone special. Smokey admired his devotion to the idea, and the more time he spent around Big Ma's place, the more he understood it.

The evening was turning to night and folks said their goodbyes and paid their respects to Big Ma for her hospitality. It was bittersweet to have the evening end, but as the night began to fall, Smokey and

Do What knew that it was time for the girls to go to work and for the liquor to start to flow.

The boys gathered the chairs and tables and carried the trash to the large trash bin behind the outhouse. They laughed and thought about how great the food and company were at these gatherings at Big Ma's. Smokey knew he had to head home at some point. His own ma would be wondering where he was, and he had to get up early to deliver his paper route.

He delivered the morning papers during the week before school, but the Sunday paper had to be delivered before 7:00 a.m., otherwise he might have his boss at the newspaper giving him a hard time. He didn't mind because he liked the people on his route. They were mostly simple folk who looked forward to their paper. Some only received the Sunday paper so he knew they would be eagerly waiting.

They heaved the last of the bags onto the trash pile and turned to head back toward Big Ma to see if there was anything else she needed help with and to thank her.

In the dim light of the porch, they spotted the man who had been searching for the congressman. The agent in his fedora was standing with Big Ma. He looked like he was asking questions. She stood with her arms folded and shook her head to most of the questions.

The boys ducked behind Ray's truck that was parked just behind the house. Smokey wanted to get closer to see if they could hear what the agent was asking Big Ma, but from where he crouched, he couldn't make out their conversation.

The man looked their way, and they ducked, hoping to avoid his glance. They didn't want to look to see if they were noticed, so they waited for a moment and then made their way behind the truck toward the front fender to see if they could peek around, almost crawling on all fours. They stopped to listen for voices, but they heard none. Curious, they started to slowly rise to see where the man had gone.

Standing right there was a tall figure hovering over them.

"What are you boys doing?" the voice said. It was Ray. The boys almost squealed in fear and relief.

"Oh man, you scared us, Ray," Smokey sighed. "We were just taking the trash to the trash pile."

"Why are you on the ground?" Ray asked.

They stuttered and scrambled to their feet. Though they tried to reach for words, nothing intelligible seemed to come out.

"The, I mean, he, I mean, Do What and I..." Smokey stuttered. He tried to notice if the agent was still talking to Big Ma, but he couldn't see around Ray, and he was afraid he might have spotted them when they first hid behind the truck.

"Who was that man?" Do What asked in a calm voice.

Ray glanced over his shoulder, but saw no one.

"What man?" Ray asked.

The boys looked over to the porch. Both Big Ma and the agent were gone.

Ray told them he had to go and asked if one of the boys might help him to take back the load of chairs he had brought from the store. Smokey needed to get going right away, and Do What agreed to help Ray as he climbed into his truck.

Smokey made his way around Big Ma's house to head toward Northfork. He figured he might hitch-hike to save some time getting back home. He walked along the road and stuck his thumb out to signal for a ride. The sky was turning darker by the minute, and Smokey was beginning to get chilled with only his short sleeve shirt and his ball cap to keep him warm.

A light shone behind him just a short distance down the road from Cinder Bottom. Smokey was relieved that he wouldn't have to walk the entire way. He raised his thumb. The bright lights blinded him, and he nearly stumbled walking backward, trying to make sure he got the driver's attention.

The car slowed and began to deliberately follow behind Smokey. The lights kept him from being able to see the car or who was in it until it was almost upon him. Smokey began to feel that there was something terribly wrong. Why was the car slowing so much but not coming up to him?

Smokey stopped and so did the car. Smokey slowly put his thumb down and tried to shield his eyes to get a look at the car and the driver. The bright headlights made it impossible to see, and Smokey decided he would turn and keep walking.

The car began to move slowly toward him.

Smokey picked up his pace and didn't look back. He could feel the car crawling slowly behind him. He wondered for a moment if he should run but decided against it. Maybe it was his stupid brother Vernon trying to mess with him. But Smokey knew that his brother's truck had dim lights, and in fact his front right headlight was out.

Smokey didn't want to let his imagination get ahead of him, but he couldn't wait to find out who it was so he stopped again, this time in the middle of the road. He waited for the car to come to him. The car stopped moving.

Smokey waited for what seemed like an eternity and the car slowly started to drive toward him. For a minute he thought it might hit him. It began to speed up slightly and then turned to go around him. He instantly recognized the car. It was the agent in his Thunderbird.

The sound of the gravel sputtered and crunched as the car drove beside him. The man kept pace with Smokey, who had started walking again.

"Need a ride?" the man asked.

"No, sir, I'm fine," Smokey replied.

He started walking slightly faster now. The car picked up its pace to keep up with him.

"Are you sure? I'm headed that way," the agent asked. "You don't want to be out here walking in the dark. You don't know who's out here and what might happen."

"I'm sure," Smokey said and continued to walk even faster.

The man didn't leave. He kept his pace with Smokey.

"I'm watching you, son, and if you have seen anyone, you better let me know," the agent said.

With that he sped off, up the road. He made a U-turn and headed back Smokey's way. For a split second, it looked as if the car was headed directly toward Smokey. He didn't flinch or leap off the road. He kept walking steadily as the car sped by him.

He wondered why the man said he was going his way when he turned around. Had he seen him and Do What at Big Ma's behind Ray's truck? The joyful afternoon barbecue at Big Ma's had almost made him forget about the agent and the missing congressman, but now that it was back in his mind, he couldn't let the idea go.

When he got home, his father was smoking on the porch and drinking a small peck of moonshine.

He stood on the porch with his father for a spell. His pa offered him a swig of his drink, and Smokey obliged him and had a sip.

"Ma kept your plate for you if you're still hungry," Father said.

"Thanks, Pa," Smokey said as he headed into the house. His mother was sitting on the small sofa and put down her sewing to look up at Smokey.

"Where you been?" Smokey's ma asked. She knew he and Do What were inseparable and figured they were out, doing what boys do. She didn't worry much but often wondered if they were getting into mischief. Smokey was prone to find trouble even if he wasn't looking for it, and once it found him, it didn't let go very easy.

"We were just hanging around today, nothing really exciting," Smokey said. With that, he stood and went to the stove and found his plate of food. Though he was pretty full from the dinner at Big Ma's, he knew she would question if he didn't eat so he sat at the table and ate his plate clean.

When he was done, he washed his plate and headed to his room.

His brother was gone, and he enjoyed not having to share the bed when he could. It wasn't that he minded, but something about having the room to himself felt like he was in his own room in another city and another world. He liked to read comics and did so when his brother wasn't there. He read the same comics over and over because he only had a few to choose from.

It was just after 9:00 p.m., and Smokey was tempted to drift off to sleep from the food that filled his belly. But he couldn't stop thinking about the congressman and the aide Peter Rose. He wondered what they might be hiding from in Cinder Bottom. He was still wondering what the agent wanted with him and why had he followed him and then tried to give him a ride.

There was something that wasn't adding up to the way the agent was acting, it was as if he was trying to find out about more than the missing congressman, but what? Smokey was certain that it wasn't as simple as a missing person, and he was determined to find out. Tomorrow after his route, he would return to the boarding house to see Lorenzo and find out if he had learned anything else. He also had a sense that Ray knew more than he let on.

All of these thoughts were in his mind and swirling around as he drifted off to sleep.

CHAPTER
5

Smokey set an alarm but usually awoke before it went off. He would start his route by folding the papers and placing them neatly in the holster bags that he carried around his shoulders. He planned to be up by 5:45 a.m. so that he could do his chores before he left. That way, he wouldn't have to return home to finish them before heading to Cinder Bottom, which was about a thirty-minute walk.

He fed the chickens and gave the slop to the pig and filled the water trough for the mule. His father usually had him working in the fields, helping prepare the land for planting or harvesting the corn. But they had tilled the soil the weekend before, and there wasn't much to do until it was time to plant again.

He wanted to have his paper route done quickly so he would have time to stop by the boarding house before meeting Do What at Geneva's. If all went well, Smokey would have his route done before 7:00 a.m.

Smokey walked his route almost on autopilot. He knew which houses wanted the paper in their paper box, which preferred to have it on the porch, and which houses had dogs that didn't like the paperboy.

He threw the papers with precision from the street and hit the porch right in front of each door with little effort. He almost never missed or lost a paper. Today, he was confident that he wouldn't need the extra paper they supplied him with, so he left it on the table for his parents who loved the Sunday paper. If he did need a paper, he had a nickel to go buy one at the corner store to replace one if it landed in a puddle or was eaten by one of the dogs that hated him. It was as if they knew he would get in trouble if they destroyed the paper.

One time Smokey was rushing to finish his route to get to the field to play ball with the brothers when he hurled a paper onto the roof of one of his customers. He realized they were not home so he thought he would get up there to retrieve the paper. He didn't want to spend the time to get his extra copy. While on the roof retrieving the paper, the ladder he had created from crates stacked against the side of the house fell. He had still been trying to get down when they arrived home to find Smokey on their roof. They hadn't been angry, but he felt a bit embarrassed because he needed them to fetch a ladder so he could get down.

His job as a paperboy was pretty uneventful most days. He never really minded the work, and it paid him weekly, which suited him. It also gave him information about what was going on because he heard all of the latest gossip and was aware of who was doing what and when. He didn't ask, but people just seemed drawn to him and would often confide in him about all sorts of things.

He once was asked to come in for a short visit by one of the young married women on his route. She offered him some sweet tea and a cookie, which sounded great to him. Once inside, the woman began to make some forward comments about how Smokey was starting to fill in as a young man, no longer the boy he once was. Smokey knew she was alone because her husband was stationed in the army in Germany. He felt uneasy, but her company was nice, and she seemed to genuinely like him. He didn't mind keeping her company but often he would be late if he stayed too long. Today, he wanted to finish early so he could head to the hotel to get as much new information from Signore Lorenzo as he could.

He finished his route just after 7:00 a.m. and was hungry. He hoped that Lorenzo had some coffee and a pastry that he usually had for Smokey. On Fridays, Smokey would bring the extra paper to Signore Lorenzo, and on Sunday he would have a coffee and treat for him. It seemed like a fair trade, and Lorenzo appreciated the early morning company.

When he was nearly at the boarding house, Smokey spotted the fancy new Thunderbird in front of the office. He looked toward Room 8 to see if Peter Rose was anywhere in sight. He looked to see if Peter's car was there, but it was gone, and the drapes to his room were drawn. Perhaps he had left and returned to Washington, or he was out and the agent was asking about Peter while he was away.

So many thoughts rushed through Smokey's mind that he almost forgot that he was headed right to the office where the agent was more than likely with Lorenzo. He got as close as he could, hiding behind the side of the building, trying to see if he could see them through the office window.

He saw the agent standing at the door, showing a piece of paper to Signore Lorenzo. It was too small and far away to make out what it was. After a short while, the agent exited the office, looked both ways, and made his way to his car. He headed down the road, and Smokey thought it was safe to go into the office. Inside, Smokey found Lorenzo dusting the antiques and singing gently to himself. The small bell rang when Smokey entered.

"Oh, Smokey, glad you made it. I just made the coffee. Come sit and let's have a bite to eat," he said, putting down his duster to grab the mugs and pour some coffee. He continued to hum, poured two cups of coffee, and placed one in front of Smokey.

Smokey took out a newspaper and placed it on the office counter.

"I had an extra paper today, signore," Smokey said.

"That's wonderful! Two papers in one week. Now that's lucky," Lorenzo said. He thanked him for the paper and sat next to Smokey, handing him the small Italian pastry that he had made for them to enjoy.

They sat in silence for a bit, something that they both felt comfortable doing. They didn't always talk. Sometimes they just sat, but today Smokey was anxious to hear what the agent was asking Lorenzo about. He needed to be sly so that Lorenzo wouldn't suspect that he was up to anything out of the ordinary.

After some comfortable silence, Smokey said casually, "That was quite some car that just left, that Thunderbird. Wow, that's a car."

"Yes, that's a nice car, not one you see here in Cinder Bottom. Big City kind of car, if you ask me," Lorenzo said. He didn't explain what the agent was doing, so Smokey knew he had to probe some if he was going to get any information from him.

He took a long sip from his coffee, shoved the last bite of his pastry in his mouth, and spoke with his mouth half full.

"Who drives that car? I've seen it around town the last few days," Smokey said.

Lorenzo hesitated then said, "He's some bigwig in D.C. looking for someone and wanted to know if I had seen him."

"Washington, D.C.?" Smokey asked innocently, hoping his curiosity would get Lorenzo to start talking more about the mysterious man.

"Yes, a long way to come for sure. He said he was done looking for the man and was headed back and wanted me to give him a call if I saw anyone suspicious or out of the ordinary. He didn't really say who he was looking for," Lorenzo said. Smokey could tell that he was not telling the whole truth.

Lorenzo, who told Smokey almost everything, felt a little odd keeping information to himself. Lorenzo was also curious about the man and who he was looking for and wanted to talk to Smokey about it, but he thought better of it. He decided to move the conversation along. He offered Smokey another pastry, which he gladly accepted, and they sipped more coffee.

Smokey wanted to ask more questions but didn't want to make Lorenzo feel uncomfortable. Smokey said that he had seen the agent and the car the day before and told Lorenzo that the man had stopped him and asked him if he had seen a man that wasn't from around there.

At this, Lorenzo felt a little better because he really wasn't telling Smokey something he didn't already know. So he opened up a bit more about his conversation with the agent.

"He said that the man was missing for three weeks and that he was certain that he was in Cinder Bottom," Lorenzo confessed.

"Why does he think he's in Cinder?" Smokey asked.

"I guess he has been coming here for a while before he disappeared," Lorenzo said.

Smokey wondered why he hadn't noticed anyone strange coming around the Bottom in the last several weeks. A stranger would be obvious, but how could he be coming to Cinder and still not be seen? And what was a junior congressman from D.C. doing in Cinder Bottom apart from drinking moonshine or looking for women? Something didn't add up.

Smokey composed himself before he asked the next question.

"Why do you think he's here in Cinder Bottom?" he asked matter-of-factly.

Lorenzo paused to sip his coffee and stared out the window as if he had been contemplating the same thing. He had a lot of time on his hands and spent most of that time alone. Besides reading, this was the only real conversation he'd had in several days.

"I think that he's been coming here for years, not weeks. He's someone we know, but just didn't know who he was from outside of Cinder," Lorenzo guessed.

That was it. He was someone that wouldn't stick out because he was actually from there. But who could he be if he was a regular in Cinder Bottom but had another life that no one knew? He'd have to be someone who was gone for long stretches of time with an alibi.

Smokey was lost in his thoughts, trying to figure out who it could be.

"More coffee?" Lorenzo asked.

Smokey had no idea how long he had been in a stupor, racking his brain trying to figure out how this person could be amongst them but still be a stranger.

"Yes, please," Smokey said. He came out of his trance and remembered that he was still in Lorenzo's company.

Lorenzo had moved on from the missing man and was talking about the change of the seasons and how much he hated the winter. Everyone in Cinder hated winter. The long cold nights and freezing days. It was only a matter of weeks, maybe even days, before the weather would turn.

Smokey was barely listening. He was still struck by the fact that the missing man was someone they all probably already knew. He was determined to figure it out but wasn't certain how all the pieces fit together.

In that moment, he remembered Peter Rose, the congressman's assistant that was staying in Room 8. He needed to know what Lorenzo knew about the man. He must be there to either cover up for him or he might be searching for him, hoping to find him before the agent did.

Smokey took another slow sip from his coffee and turned to Lorenzo. "Have you noticed anyone unusual here, Lorenzo?" he asked. He didn't want to seem like he was digging, but he wanted to know what Lorenzo could tell him about Peter. "I thought I saw a strange car here with D.C. plates the other day." Smokey tried to act as if it was a perfectly logical question to ask.

Lorenzo turned to him and squinched up his face. "Now that you mention it, there was a man here from D.C. for a few days," he said. "He was a nervous young fella that seemed out of place. But he wasn't here long."

Smokey remembered that Lorenzo said that Peter would leave in the middle of the night and wondered if that had anything to do with the missing congressman. Lorenzo almost never missed what was going on in Cinder Bottom. Though he had a house, he often slept on a cot in the back office because he didn't have help to watch the place overnight. On a few occasions, Smokey had watched the office when Lorenzo had to make a trip uptown to Bluefield to handle some banking or other business. He wondered how Lorenzo made it by himself, managing the place since his mother died. He seemed content yet he was still alone.

Smokey understood how important his visits were to Lorenzo. It was as if the entire town didn't see him, but Smokey did. Smokey appreciated his humor, his Italian records, and his simple life. Being with Lorenzo reminded Smokey that there were still exotic places like Italy out there. Lorenzo also longed to travel but had fallen into being the caretaker of the lodging that his mother left him. It was as if she still dwelled there; if he let it go, she might be gone too. His Italian was starting to feel like it was a distant memory, and anything he could do to keep a hold on the old country and his mother was all that mattered.

Smokey was pondering this when he noticed Peter Rose's car pulled up in the parking lot. He wasn't sure at first but when he saw the man get out of his car with his starched collared button-down shirt and round glasses, he was certain it was him. Smokey thought of asking Lorenzo about the car and about Peter, but before he could, the man came walking into the office. The bell rang and Lorenzo stood at attention to greet him.

"Good morning, sir. Welcome back. How may I help you?" Lorenzo said. The man looked around and noticed Smokey but said nothing.

"Hello, sir, I would like a room for one more night," he said. He seemed nervous.

"Of course, sir, would you like Room 8 again?" Lorenzo asked.

"That would be fine," the man said.

"Yes, of course, just one moment," Lorenzo said as he made his way behind the office desk to get the man checked in. Smokey noticed that he had nice oxford shoes and was wearing a wedding ring. He also noticed that he had the morning paper from Bluefield. He couldn't make out the entire headline, but he could see that part of it had the word Congress on it. Smokey assumed it was about the missing congressman and figured he would go to Ray's to see if he could get the paper from Bluefield from him. The man took the keys, paid in cash, and left. Lorenzo looked at Smokey as if to say, "I guess there's more to learn here than we thought." He had hoped that the man might leave a clue as to what he was doing there and to help uncover who the mystery man was. Smokey knew he had to find a picture of the congressman so he could figure out what he was doing in Cinder Bottom. There had to be a back issue of the Bluefield Daily Telegraph that had his picture.

"Lorenzo, has that man been here for long?" Smokey said. He knew he had seen him before and just wanted him to confirm that.

"Yes, he was here the last few days." Lorenzo said. "He's been coming here for a month."

Smokey realized that he was not aware of how long this might have been going on. He only really started to pay attention when he first overheard the agent and the sheriff's conversation. Lorenzo probably had been trying to piece everything together for weeks. If he was going to figure out what was going on, he needed to know what Lorenzo knew. Had the agent asked him questions and then told him not to say anything?

"Do you know why he's here?" Smokey asked.

"No, not really, except that he was asking about a girl. Someone who was supposed to be at Big Ma's place. That's all I know," Lorenzo said.

Big Ma's place? Who was the girl and what did she have to do with Big Ma? Now Smokey was energized to get more information. He thanked Lorenzo for the coffee and pastry and got his shoulder bag for his papers. Lorenzo thanked him for the paper and said he hoped to see him soon.

Smokey left and headed to Ray's to see if he was back from his run to Bluefield and to see if he had the paper from Sunday. He hoped that there would be a picture of the congressman that might give him a clue as to who he was and why he was around Cinder Bottom. What Smokey couldn't figure out was why Peter was asking about a girl from Big Ma's place. Which girl might he be talking about, and what did that have to do with Peter or the congressman? There were too many unanswered questions, and Smokey needed to get some answers.

Smokey had plans to meet Do What at Geneva's. He would tell him what he found out. Then, after they ate a bite, they could head over to Ray's to see if they could get the paper. When it was a decent hour, he would head over to Big Ma's to see if he could figure out who Peter might be looking for.

When Smokey got to Geneva's, Do What was already there talking to a girl that they went to elementary school with.

When they were young, most of the girls teased and made fun of Do What. However, this girl had always been kind to Do What. Nancy was always kind and thoughtful toward him. She treated him like a younger brother, even though they were the same age. She never let anyone pick on him or make fun of him. She saw something in him that no one else saw, that he was smart and deep in an altruistic way. She appreciated that Do What didn't have a judgmental bone in his body and always saw the bright side of things, even though his family life was a mess.

Nancy had cherry-blonde curly hair and blue eyes that seemed to always be bright. Nancy had recently moved back to Cinder Bottom after being gone for nearly five years. Her father was a foreman at the mines and they lived in a big house just outside of town. She could have been a snob, being what most people in town would consider a rich kid. Smokey was always attracted to her smile and sweet innocence, but he never let on that he liked her because he didn't want to make Do What jealous in any way.

One time when they were in elementary school, Smokey walked her home after school. When Do What found out, he didn't talk to Smokey for almost a month. Smokey knew that even though there wasn't anything that he could see that was romantic about Do What and Nancy's relationship, he should never come between them. Do What saw her as a prized friend, and apart from Smokey, Nancy was the only person he felt he could be open with.

Smokey stayed back for a bit to see if they were going to talk for long because he didn't want to interrupt. It looked like she was just leaving, though, and soon Do What was sitting alone. Nancy had waved sweetly to Do What as she left, and he waved back and stared after she was long gone.

Smokey sat down next to him and sat in silence as he stared after her.

"How's Nancy?" Smokey asked, trying to break the trance. Do What was still staring and didn't respond until Smokey placed his hand on his shoulder.

"Oh, hey Smoke, didn't see you there," Do What said coming out of his stupor. "You hungry? I'm starving. Let's get some chow."

They rose and went to the counter to order some food. They ordered coffee and a large helping of biscuits and gravy to share.

Waiting for the food to arrive, Smokey told Do What about the agent, Peter Rose, and the girl that might help them figure out why the congressman might be in Cinder Bottom.

Do What listened intently but didn't say a word, shoveling large helpings of biscuits and gravy into his mouth followed by gulps of hot coffee.

"Did you notice on your way here if Ray's truck was in the back of the store?" Smokey asked.

"Nope, didn't see it parked there yet," he said.

Do What continued to eat but was slowing now.

Smokey hardly had a bite or two of biscuits because he was so preoccupied with trying to keep track of all of the details of this mystery. If he could see what the congressman looked like, it might trigger his memory to remember who he was. It would be hard for anyone that came from Cinder Bottom to become a congressman without the whole town knowing.

So, what was the tie that this man had to Cinder, what did the girl have to do with this, and why was he missing? There were so many missing pieces that it was starting to give Smokey a headache trying to solve the puzzle. Why would Peter be looking for a girl at Big Ma's place and what could she have to do with the missing congressman?

He sipped his coffee and pushed his serving of biscuits toward Do What, who gladly devoured them.

They had the same thing every Sunday. Geneva paid the boys for the work that they did in trade: biscuits and gravy each week that they worked. It wasn't a lot, but it suited them just fine.

When they finished, they thanked Geneva and headed out to see if Ray had returned from his weekly run to Bluefield. There was no sign of him yet, so they decided to sit on the back porch to wait for his arrival.

Smokey replayed all of the details that they already knew. They saw the agent first on Friday, before the ballgame. Smokey was confronted by him when he went back to get the moonshine and the brothers all headed to the miner's house. They had then seen him at Lorenzo's, Ray's, and finally, Big Ma's. He was making his rounds to see if anyone saw anything, but something didn't add up.

If everyone that Smokey knew told him they hadn't seen anyone, why was he still looking? It was as if he wanted them to think they had seen him or at least to get them to talk about seeing him. What if he had never been there at all, but the agent wanted them to all start to wonder if he was in their midst? That would be virtually impossible for everyone not to notice such a famous congressman, especially one that was in the paper in Bluefield. If he wasn't there, why was Peter Rose there pretending to be someone else? What was he doing in Cinder Bottom and why was he not in Washington?

There were too many holes in this story, and it was starting to bug Smokey that he couldn't figure out what was going on.

CHAPTER
6

Ray pulled up as the boys were running through the events yet again. He drove a 1949 Chevy truck that was his pride and joy. It wasn't perfect but it purred like a kitten. Ray had it washed each week, even though the roads in Cinder Bottom were filthy with coal dust. No matter how hard anyone tried, things collected a coat of soot, leaving everything with a gray hue.

Coal dust was pervasive to life in the coalfields. They referred to the Elkhorn River as "The Black Creek" because the water flowed past each of the mining operations where they "washed" the coal. This process sent all the loose black dust into the stream. The nasty soot tended to make things like rugs, curtains, and other textiles sticky and left a distinctive tar-like scent on anything it touched.

Once Ray parked, the boys immediately began to help him unload. They took the supplies and stacked them just outside the back door on the porch. He had canned foods, flour, rice, beans, soda pop, kitchen supplies, and a few other sundries.

When they finished, Ray was sweating and almost out of breath. He was a large man, almost six feet tall and in good shape, but his weight always seemed to get the best of him. He always said that between Geneva's biscuits and gravy and Big Ma's barbecue, it would be the death of him. Ray loved to eat as much as he loved to read and gossip, which often went hand-in-hand depending on who was involved.

Ray returned to his truck, reached in, and grabbed the Sunday edition of the *Bluefield Daily Telegraph*. He handed it to Smokey.

"You can have the whole thing, not just the comics today. I already finished it. Got some good stuff in there this week," Ray said.

Smokey thanked him, and he and Do What sat down to scan the front page for headlines.

The top lead read, "Junior Congressman Found." Do What and Smokey stared at each other and gasped. They opened the page that covered the story.

The congressman had deliberately been avoiding Capitol Hill as an act of protest to Senator Byrd's Manifesto and the massive resistance to the Brown case that called for desegregation of public schools. According to the article, he had been hiding out due to some threats on his life. He was one of only a few Republican candidates in the South that refused to support a movement to withhold state funds for any schools that allowed colored students to attend white schools. He was returning to Washington to make a public appearance about his decision and what his next steps were in response to the events that had occurred.

There were no pictures of the congressman, but the headline had a photo of the protestors that staged sit-ins and marches across the South.

Now Smokey and Do What were even more confused. If the congressman wasn't missing and had instead been hiding out, why were they trying to say he was in Cinder Bottom? Was he really hiding out there, or was there another reason the agent was in Cinder Bottom?

"Do What, why do you think the agent was making it so obvious he was looking for someone? Do you think he actually told Lorenzo, Ray, or Big Ma who he was looking for?" Smokey asked.

Do What shrugged and didn't say a word, except to ask Smokey for the comics section. Smokey gladly gave them to him, because he knew that he would be dropping them off to the girls at Big Ma's after they were done with the paper.

Do What read the comics and laughed to himself at times while Smokey just sat in contemplation. He had almost decided to give up on figuring out any more details about the agent or the congressman when he noticed a small article buried in the last section of the page he had been reading. It read, "Theodore aka

'Buddy' Myers, President of the Myers Coal and Coke Company, Said to Be Under Investigation."

Buddy Myers, Nancy Myers's dad, the nice girl that adored Do What, was being investigated for misconduct and money laundering. Smokey was glad that Do What was distracted by the comics and hadn't seen the article. He would have been upset and angry that such a claim could be made. The Myers family were known to be good people, but the Myers Mine was where Do What's dad had been injured. They had refused to pay any compensation for his fathers' injury, calling it a worker error.

If he had been given any compensation, his family wouldn't be in such a tough spot. His mom had to work two jobs just to get food on the table, and his brother, Mike, was a drunk and almost as useless when it came to working. Mike had several jobs but got fired from all of them. His father also drank, and the only thing that kept Do What halfway sane was that he had Smokey to distract him. Being a coal miner was a good job if you didn't get killed while doing it or develop black lung that killed you when you were done working.

Do What finished reading the paper and handed it back to Smokey. He sat back on the porch, leaning on his elbows grinning.

"Smokey, Beetle Bailey gets into all kinds of mischief. He's kind of like us, I suppose," Do What said matter-of-factly.

"I guess you're right," Smokey said. It was too early for his brain to be this tired. He had to clear his mind and think of what all of this new information was leading to. He wanted to tell Do What about the Myers scandal but figured he would learn about it for himself soon enough.

He rolled up the paper and rose from the porch, motioning for Do What to follow.

They headed toward Big Ma's. It was a bit early for anyone to be up, but he figured it might be worth the shot. At the very least, he could drop the comics off for the girls and come back later to talk to Big Ma.

Smokey wondered whether he should head for Lorenzo's after and outright tell him what he was thinking. He might be able to help him piece it together. But what if there wasn't anything really wrong? What if the agent wasn't looking for the congressman but was looking for someone else? There were too many unanswered questions, and he needed to find out what Big Ma knew before he made any other moves.

Smokey's teacher would say that he was too smart for his own good and often would tell him to stop asking questions if she didn't know the answers. He tolerated school because his friends were there. Being at school allowed him to play ball and talk to girls— both were very high on his priority list.

Still, he would have liked it more if his teachers didn't ignore his questions, which to him seemed very pertinent and logical. They just told him that he was being a nuisance and trying to get them flustered, which was partially true. He just couldn't help himself.

If he wanted to know something, he had to figure it out. It was like a raccoon who got a hold of a shiny object—he didn't let it go no matter what might be at stake. It was, in fact, how coon hunters might trap a racoon. They placed a shiny object in a hole with nails pointing downward at an angle that made it easy for a small hand or paw to fit in and out. If you made a fist, your paw or hand wouldn't be able to get out. To get free, all the racoons needed to do was to release the object, but they usually refused to let go. With a trap like this, dogs got close enough to tree a coon, which is how the hunters then got the raccoon in the end.

When they arrived at Big Ma's, the doors and windows were still shut and the evidence of a late night was made clear by the bottles of trash strewn across the parking area.

Smokey and Do What started to pick up the litter and take it to the rubbish pile, something they would usually do. It was one of the reasons that Big Ma took good care of those boys; they were never told to help around the place, they usually just did.

Big Ma treated them like relatives and that suited them fine, because they loved the Saturday evening barbecues and the familiar way the girls treated them when they came by. Their friends thought it was strange that they liked to hang out at Big Ma's place, but Smokey and Do What didn't care what they thought; they liked their adopted family.

When they finished picking up the trash, there still was no sign of any life inside the house, so the boys placed the paper near the door and decided they would come back a bit later.

Smokey remembered that he saw the agent also speaking to Geneva and wondered if she might give him some information about the agent. What he wanted to know was whether they were all being asked or told the same thing.

When Smokey had overheard the agent speaking to the sheriff, he heard him asking about a stranger who was possibly in Cinder Bottom. Smokey had just assumed that the agent was looking for the missing congressman. But what if Smokey had been wrong the whole time? What if it was just a coincidence that the congressman was missing, and that the agent was looking for someone else? Things weren't adding up. Why was Peter Rose there if he wasn't there to find the congressman? He was an aide after all. Maybe Smokey needed to figure out what Peter was doing there and why he had been using a fake name at Lorenzo's.

On the way to Geneva's, Smokey and Do What ran into the brothers: Larry, Bob, and Sam. They were up early for those hooligans, and Smokey wondered what they were up to.

"Hey, fellas," Smokey said.

They all in unison said, "Hey."

"We're hunting stills today. You wanna come help?" Bob asked.

The brothers took great pleasure in hunting the moonshine stills that were littered throughout the county. They knew it was a dangerous sport and could even get them killed, but it was the hunt that they liked. They had found several, but they still bought their moonshine from the Farmers on Friday's. They would never try to steal any of the liquor. It was just fun to try to hunt and not get caught. One time, Do What's older brother was found trying to steal some liquor from a still. If it wasn't for his dad's injury, the shiners would have probably killed him.

The brothers were all eager to go hunting today, and they weren't gonna take no for an answer. Normally, Smokey would be excited to go, but today it felt like a distraction from the puzzle he was turning over in his head.

There wasn't a discussion; they all just started to head out of town toward the nearest holler that they had suspected might be a good spot for a still. There was a spring about two hundred yards up that would be a perfect supply of water.

The holler was too narrow to make it easy to get to except by foot. The hills on each side made it possible for only one entrance, which meant it would be easier to defend if the Feds or someone else came looking for it. They knew there was another way around the holler by way of a deer trail that led right to the spring. If they were careful, they might find a still. With the mist and fog still hanging over the hills, it would make for perfect cover if the moonshiner's were cooking their mash, since the smoke would blend into the fog.

They hiked in silence; they knew that they had to imagine that they were already being watched and had to act innocent yet move with caution. The deer trail was clearly marked, but there were still some difficult areas that they had to crawl on their hands and knees to get through. Larry, usually the leader in these expeditions, was out front blazing the trail.

They were nearing the ridge where the spring was thought to be when Larry raised his fist as a silent indication that they should all freeze in their tracks. They ducked down and waited for the next signal, which might be to turn and run or to proceed with caution. The suspense was killing them, yet this is the feeling they longed for, the excitement of not knowing what might happen next.

They could see Larry crouching down but couldn't make out what he was looking at. He seemed puzzled and uncertain whether he should signal them to come or to turn and run.

The air was still cool and the only sounds they could make out were the gentle sound of the spring bubbling out of the ground and the fall leaves rustling above. They hid right above the spring.

The still had to be close by and maybe there was someone already there. Larry turned to shush them and then signaled them to come quietly. The brothers crept on their hands and knees until they were caught up with Larry. What they saw was not what they expected.

They had, in fact, found a still. It was just a short distance away from their vantage point, and they could make out all of the details from there. This morning, the still was being used for other purposes. There were two large men, standing over a large sack with rifles in their hands.

When Sam saw the guns, he almost gasped. Larry shushed him and placed a hand over his mouth. They were so close that they were afraid that even heavy breathing might give them away.

CHAPTER
7

The large sack at their feet was long and bulky. The men seemed to be contemplating what to do with it. The usual smell of the sour mash that was used to make moonshine was not apparent, though the still seemed to be running.

Sam, who was almost always impatient, was ready to go; he had enough of this quiet game, and now that they had found the moonshine, he had no interest in what these men were doing or what might be in the burlap bag. He had not had anything to eat, and he was growing weary of waiting. His stomach started to turn and make the familiar but disturbing sounds of an empty stomach. It was so loud that Larry turned to hush it.

Sam rolled his eyes and pointed to his stomach. Larry and the other boys rolled their eyes and turned back to the still to see what was going on.

One of the men below was not much older than they were, maybe eighteen or nineteen, but they were large-framed and strong. The veins in his muscular arms appeared whenever he clenched the rifle, giving away the tension he must have been feeling.

The other man was smaller in stature. He wore a fedora like the agent and didn't seem to mind the weight of the gun in his hand. He seemed confident and assured about what they were doing.

Smokey wanted to get closer to see if he could make out their faces and hear what they were saying. From their current distance, the bubbling sound of the spring drowned out their voices and made it almost impossible to make out a single word.

He signaled to Larry that he was going in for a closer look. Larry's eyes expressed his disapproval, or at least his hesitation, but he nodded back to him.

Bob was getting nervous. The fun was over and the men with guns were enough to spook him. He had been caught sneaking around a still once before and didn't want to be shot at again. The last time had been too close for his liking. He slowly started to back away from the ledge that the boys were spying from.

Smokey traced his steps backward to make his way around the ledge to get a bit closer and farther from the sounds of the spring. He moved stealthily and didn't attract any attention to himself.

As he knelt behind a large tree, he could hear the men speaking.

"What are we gonna do with him?" asked the younger man.

"I dunno. We were just supposed to get him and bring him here and wait," said the other man in a stern voice.

Smokey recognized the man's voice. It had a distinct sound to it. It was gruff and sharp, but definitely not from McDowell County or maybe not even from West Virginia. He had a city sound to his voice.

"Don't get cold feet now," the man said.

Smokey was certain that he had heard that voice before and wanted to get a closer look. He crawled his way to a tree that was just out of sight from the still. Now that he was farther away from the spring, he could clearly hear their voices.

"I ain't got cold feet. I'm just wondering how long we need to stay here," the younger man said.

Smokey recognized the voice now: it sounded like it might be Jacob, the oldest of the Farmer boys who had sold Smokey the moonshine.

The young man seemed a bit nervous and tense, even for a moonshiner. He started to pace a bit. With the rifle on his hip, he started to kick at the sack at their feet.

Smokey finally caught a glimpse of the boy's face. As he suspected, it was Jacob for sure, but Smokey still couldn't make out the face of the man in the hat. He was blocked by the still, and the angle from where Smokey stood and the man's hat made it hard to see his face. But something about him seemed familiar. He just couldn't place the voice.

"There's no telling how long we are gonna have to wait. You gotta keep calm," the man said.

He partially turned in the direction that Smokey was standing, and Smokey almost got a glimpse of the man. He thought if he just got a little closer, he would be able to see him. He glanced over to where Larry was.

Larry sent a sharp "no" with his eyes to Smokey. He could see that Sam and Bob were already inching backward to make their way back down the holler.

Smokey turned back toward the still and crept a bit closer to the pacing men below.

"I ain't gotta good feeling about this. What if someone saw us?" the Farmer boy said.

"Don't cha worry about it none. No one saw us, and no one knows where we are so don't worry," the man said.

That's when Smokey remembered where he had heard that voice: it was Peter Rose, from Signore Lorenzo's place. He was certain because of what he said, "Don't cha worry about it none." He knew it was him, and the fedora he was wearing was the same one he had seen the day he saw him entering Room 8. He searched for Do What as to confirm what he saw, but there was no sign of him.

Larry signaled to Smokey that he was heading back down the holler. Smokey stood listening to see if he could make out any more of their conversation, but Bob, who was as clumsy as an ox, tripped over a large rock that broke free and tumbled down the hill toward the spring.

Smokey froze, and so did the other boys.

Peter and the Farmer boy turned, looking for the source of the noise. The rock rolled all the way down the hill and settled at their feet. They aimed the rifle in the direction of the brothers and waited. They stood in silence and so did the brothers. Smokey's chest was heaving, and he breathed deeper.

In that moment, a blackbird rose and took flight right over the brothers' heads. The Farmer boy aimed toward the bird and with a nervous impulse, fired his rile, missing the bird by several yards.

"You idiot! Someone will hear that," Peter said, using his hand to lower the boy's rifle. "There's no one there. It was just a bird."

The Farmer boy seemed to know that a bird wouldn't cause a rock to roll down the hill, but he wanted to believe it was nothing and relented and lowered his gun.

Larry and the boys exhaled and continued to creep backward down the hill.

Smokey, who was now almost in Peter and the boy's sight, stayed frozen in place, not wanting to be seen.

The Farmer boy and Peter turned back toward the large sack, and Smokey tried to get a better look at what it might contain. What could possibly be inside a sack so large? He noticed that the sack seemed to be moving, almost squirming.

"See what you did? You woke her up," Peter said. "You are gonna get us killed."

The Farmer boy turned and gave the sack a slight kick. Peter pushed his feet away.

"Nothing can harm her, you understand?" Peter said. "She's worth more than you and your entire family is dead or alive, so you better settle down."

Her? Smokey wondered. What or who was in the sack was the new source of Smokey's curiosity. It was as if he didn't have any fear that these men might shoot him. His curiosity was in overdrive, and he had to know what the congressman's aide had to do with the Farmers and who or what was in the sack. He had more questions now than when he first started chasing this crazy story down.

Smokey could no longer see the brothers. They had traveled so far down the holler that they were out of sight. Smokey knew if he stayed too much longer, he might be seen. But Smokey had that same fire of adrenaline in his veins when he first started to question the congressman's disappearance and why he might be in Cinder Bottom. Too many questions still lingered in his mind, and he would not stop until he had more answers. His raccoon nature just couldn't drop the shiny object that he had in his grasp, even if that might mean he might already be in a trap, or worse, caught.

What was Peter Rose doing with a Farmer boy in the holler by a moonshine still, and what was in the sack? Smokey kept trying to make the connection to Cinder Bottom, the congressman, and now to Peter Rose. Smokey had thought that perhaps Peter was in Cinder also looking for the congressman, like the agent. But he also thought that perhaps Peter was there to keep the congressman's whereabouts a secret. That maybe he knew where he was and what he was doing in Cinder Bottom. But when the congressman returned to Washington, and Peter Rose stayed at Lorenzo's, Smokey thought that maybe he was wrong about his speculation. He wondered why Peter was there.

Smokey's mind was doing somersaults trying to create a new story about what he had discovered.

The sack below was now motionless again, and the boy and Peter were not on high alert at the moment. Smokey needed to know what was in the sack. He couldn't stand not knowing, and he would wait as long as he needed to find out. He knew the brothers would be long gone down the holler by then and would be too far away to do anything if something should happen. If Peter and Jacob noticed him, he would be shot for sure. Smokey didn't plan on that happening, but he still had it in the back of his mind.

Smokey moved farther away from their line of sight but where he could still watch their movements. He saw Jacob and Peter having an intense discussion about the sack because they kept pointing at it and then gesturing back down the holler and then back at the sack. Peter finally threw his hands in the air, handed the Farmer boy his rifle, and headed down the holler.

The boy leaned the rifle on the still and began to shout in Peter's direction. The only thing that Smokey could make out was, "You better get back soon! I ain't waiting up here all day!"

Smokey kept a close eye on Jacob but stayed out of sight. After pacing for a bit, he set his rifle down by his side and sat on a log that made for a nice stool just a few feet away from the sack. He was fidgeting and bouncing his leg.

Smokey knew he had no chance of figuring out this mystery with Jacob sitting so close by. The rifle also gave him pause. Smokey wondered if he would grow weary of waiting for Peter and would just leave, but knew that was unlikely. Whatever was in the sack was worth protecting or they wouldn't be hiding it. If Smokey could distract the boy long enough, he could make his way down to look in the sack. Smokey couldn't walk away like the other brothers had done. He wished he was less curious, but he just couldn't go without finding out what was in the sack.

Smokey remembered that each moonshiner often hid supplies, weapons, and even cash near their stills, just in case they were raided or if thieves came to steal from the shiners and they had to make a hasty getaway. The supplies were in case they had to make their way farther into the woods to escape capture, the weapons to defend themselves. And the cash to aid in their getaway. This stash was often protected by an unsuspecting booby trap that would stop or maim trespassers if they attempted to raid the concealed stockpile.

Smokey knew that it wasn't a good idea to try to attack an armed person, but if he had a weapon too, perhaps he could fire in the direction of Jacob. His goal wasn't to harm him. He just hoped he could get him to run away.

But what if the plan failed and the boy shot back at him? That plan was not going to work. Besides, he would first have to locate the supposed stash and then find a way to scare the boy away.

Smokey was growing impatient and was frustrated not to have a plan or even another idea yet. He wished that Do What was there. He always seemed to come up with something unexpected and useful in moments like these. That's the kind of person he was: quiet, pensive, and unsuspecting. But Smokey was alone, and he had to be careful with his next move.

His logical brain told him to quietly sneak back down the holler, forget what he saw, and be grateful he didn't get shot. But his curious brain was in full force, and he was on a mission to figure out this crazy puzzle that he had been trying to solve. He wanted to leave McDowell County and go see the world, but for now this was the most excitement he had in his entire life. The idea of big city agents and Washington congressmen being tied to Cinder Bottom was just too alluring to him. He was already this far down the path that he didn't want to go back now.

Smokey thought that perhaps he would try to get to a different vantage point to see better. He took his first step but then froze when he heard what he thought was a gunshot from off in the distance further up the holler. Smokey waited to see what might have caused the sound. If it were a gun, it was from someone who was already further up the holler.

The Farmer boy rose to his feet and grabbed his rifle. He aimed up the holler in the direction of the sound.

"Who's there?" the boy shouted.

But there was only the echo of the gunshot wailing through the mountains. He looked back down the holler and then back up the holler and then down at the sack. He called again.

"I said, who's there?" he shouted.

Nothing.

He took a few steps toward the sound of the gunshot and took slow steps aiming at any hint of noise. He was shaking and aiming the gun in every direction. Forgetting the sack, the boy headed up the holler, making his way up the side of the mountain in the direction of the gunshot. It was hard to tell where it really came from because of the echo.

Smokey waited to see how far up the holler the Farmer Boy would go. He was nearly out of sight, and Smokey thought that perhaps he was far enough away that he might be able to sneak down and look inside of the bag. He knew it was risky. What if Peter was just a short distance away? He would have heard the gunshot and perhaps was already headed back.

The boy continued until he was out of sight. Smokey decided to take his chance.

He started down from his hiding spot to see if he could peek into the sack, which remained motionless near the still. Smokey made his way closer to the sack, trying to keep track of the boy as well as look down the holler in the direction that Peter went, so he could quickly escape if there was any sign of either of them. He was within yards of the sack. He could sense the tension growing as he got closer and closer.

When he was nearly five feet away, another gunshot sounded, and Smokey froze. He couldn't move. He was petrified with fear that the Farmer boy had spotted him. He checked himself over and saw that he was unharmed. When he was sure he didn't see Jacob or Peter anywhere nearby, he continued on.

Smokey was nearly at the sack when it moved, and he jumped back. Committed to knowing what was in the sack, Smokey continued. When he reached the sack, he heard a faint groan. In that moment he heard a loud yell and thud up the holler, then there was silence. Had the Farmer boy fallen? Had someone hit him? Smokey couldn't waste time on speculation. He untied the top of the sack to reveal finally what was inside.

At first, he only saw darkness, as if the sack was filled with black wool. Smokey reached toward the sack to try to reveal what was inside.

In the distance, Smokey heard footsteps coming from the direction that Jacob had gone. There was no time to head back up to his hiding spot or he would be detected and perhaps shot. He cinched the top of the sack closed and scrambled to the backside of the still to hide. He held his breath waiting for Jacob to return.

Maybe the boy had shot whatever had made the noise and was now headed back. He thought about running down the holler, hoping he might be able to outrun the boy and dive into the brush to avoid being an open target for his rifle. If he had killed or injured whoever was in the woods with a gun, he could certainly hurt or kill him. But Smokey had hesitated too long. He decided to hide right where he was rather than risk being caught in the open.

Though he couldn't see the path that the Farmer boy's footsteps were coming from, he could hear them getting louder and louder. By now the approaching figure would be in sight of his hiding place. He remembered something his grandmother would say: the Lord knows what the devil does, and it does him no good to hide. He was hoping that the Lord would make an exception this time. He wasn't a church goer nor was he a praying man, but he hoped that the Lord was at least willing to give him a second chance to get away.

The sound of the footsteps grew louder and louder, which meant he was almost to where he was hiding. Smokey crouched down behind the still. He could now see the feet of the Farmer boy, and the butt of the rifle was resting on the ground beside him. Smokey tried to remember to breathe, but not too deeply to draw attention to his hiding spot.

He wondered whether he could use the element of surprise if the boy were to turn away from him. Maybe he could get him to drop the gun. But the more Smokey tried to envision doing this, the more it seemed like one of his comics and even more far-fetched than the predicament he had already got himself into.

His father always told Smokey not to do stupid things. He would say, "Now, son, keep your mind on what you're doin' right here (meaning during tricky moments and other volatile situations). If you ain't careful, you'll get your dick knocked up in your watch pocket." A funny way of saying that would be quite an unwanted situation to be in, so don't do it. Or, given the current unwanted situation, pay close attention to what you do next and don't go gettin' shot at or killed.

Smokey let the idea of jumping on the Farmer boy go but was now stuck hiding almost in plain sight. If the boy turned and looked his way under the still, his feet and legs would be sure to give him away.

Smokey wanted to run, but he had nowhere to go. He wanted to step out and say he was just trying to figure out what was in the sack. He didn't care what Peter and Jacob were up to—Smokey just wanted to know. He would say his curiosity got the best of him and he was sorry that he stumbled on to the still and the hiding spot, that he didn't mean to cause a problem.

But Smokey knew it was too late and that he was in deeper than he wanted to be. As Jacob's feet got closer and closer, he could feel the tension grow. The boy's feet froze right in front of him, and Smokey's heart stopped. Would this be the end of his short life because he wouldn't let his curiosity go?

But the Farmer boy didn't move, he just stood there. Why wouldn't he just get it over with, aim the gun at Smokey, and shoot him already? Smokey was certain he had been discovered and that the boy knew he was behind the still. Why did he make him suffer by waiting?

Smokey contemplated what his mother would say, what might be said at his funeral. He was a good kid, but his curiosity killed him. He wouldn't just let it be, he had to dig deeper and find out what was going on, and that is what killed him.

His mind raced. Why was he not yet dead? Why would he not just forget about the congressman, Peter, and the sack? Why was he constantly obsessed with knowing what was going on? He was often in some sort of mischief and he wanted to vow that he would never again let curiosity get the best of him, but the moment he thought it, he knew it was a lie.

Jacob moved closer to where he was hiding, and Smokey knew that he was going to die.

"Smokey? Is that you?" a voice said.

Smokey recognized this voice; it was Do What. Smokey rose from behind the still.

"Do What?" he said. "What the hell are you doing here? What happened to Jacob?"

Do What stood over the now-wriggling sack.

"When you all took off up the holler, I was watchin' the hawks above the ravine and lost track of you and the brothers," Do What said. "I realized you were up there trapped. I caused a commotion up at the hideout where there was a rifle."

He went on to explain that the Farmer boy had come to see where the gunfire had come from. When Jacob walked up the holler, he fell in the trap that was left for any thieves coming to steal the moonshine. The second shot discharged from Jacob's rifle when he fell and it hit the ground.

Smokey was relieved to see Do What. He had no idea how much time they had before Peter came back or if the Farmer boy might climb out of the trap somehow.

Smokey immediately went to the sack to open it. He bent down and uncinched the large burlap sack.

When he opened it, a small black puppy yawned and crawled out.

This was not what he was expecting. Why would they be willing to risk their life for a dog? Now Smokey was more confused than ever. Why did Peter and the boy have a puppy up at the still, and why was it worth more than their lives to protect?

Once again, Smokey and Do What were scratching their heads trying to understand. Smokey bent down and studied the tag hanging from her collar. It read: "For Ruby."

The puppy licked and squirmed its way on to Smokey's lap.

The boys heard rustling down below in the holler. Smokey quickly put the puppy back in the sack and tied it just enough to keep it from escaping. They left the sack where they had found it and ran for cover.

The puppy was whimpering now. The boys tried to hush it from afar but grew quiet once they saw Peter walking up with a brown paper bag.

"Jacob?" Peter shouted.

No reply.

The puppy's whimpering made it hard to hear anything else.

"Jacob, where are you?" he yelled again.

With the Farmer boy out of sight, Peter noticed the rifle left leaning on the still. He grabbed it and started up the holler. "That damn boy better not have run off," he said. He continued calling Jacob's name and aiming the rifle at any noise.

The puppy squirmed and the knot had started to come loose. The boys knew that if the puppy got loose, it might give up their hiding spot.

Meanwhile, Jacob had finally been able to crawl out of the booby-trapped hole left for thieves and headed down to the still where he encountered Peter.

"What are you doing up here, and why the hell are you so dirty?" Peter barked.

Jacob was covered in leaves and dirt from falling into the pit.

"You left Ruby alone. What on earth is wrong with you?"

"I heard a gunshot, so I went to go find out who it was, then I fell in a trap," Jacob said. Peter was not certain he was buying this story since there didn't seem to be any reason for a gunshot to go off.

"It was probably just the wind or something. Besides, I told you not to leave Ruby alone," Peter said.

"It's just a damn dog," Jacob said.

"It's not just a dog, and you need to follow directions. When I say stay here and watch Ruby, I mean it," Peter said.

They were arguing and weren't noticing the sack slowly beginning to unravel as the knot came undone. The sack wiggled and flipped back and forth and a small tuft of fur could be seen at the opening. A few more wiggles and the puppy would be free.

Do What and Smokey started to back away from their hiding spot. They knew if that dog got loose, it would make its way to them and give up their location. They had only a moment before the puppy would break free.

Jacob and Peter continued to argue and were not aware of the escape artist they had on their hands.

Smokey and Do What were finally far enough away from the moonshine still that they could get up and start to run away the way they had come, quietly and with their heads down. They ran as fast as they could go, trying to stay out of any clearing for fear Peter and Jacob might spot them. They arrived at the bottom of the holler and stopped to catch their breath.

"That was close," Smokey said. Do What nodded in agreement.

Just when they thought they had made it free, they heard what they thought sounded like a gunshot.

"Jacob, what are you doing, you idiot? Someone will hear you," Peter yelled. Jacob had heard the rustling of the boys escape and thought he would scare the potential intruder. In that moment, the puppy had finally worked her way loose. When the gun went off, the dog took off running in the direction of the boys.

"Look what you did! The dog got away!" Peter shouted. "Go after it!"

Jacob dropped the rifle and grabbed the sack. He started running in the direction of the dog, but he was limping from his fall into the pit. The dog was fast, and Jacob was not able to catch up before it disappeared into the brush.

Peter threw his rifle down in disgust and threw his hands into the air, watching both the dog and Jacob disappear into the trees.

The puppy picked up Do What and Smokey's scent and ran down the holler toward the boys.

When the gunshot went off, the boys had started to run again. They didn't wait to see what the commotion was about. Smokey and Do What ran as fast as they had ever run, and they were nearly back down to the main road when they came across the rest of the brothers sitting on a log. When the brothers heard the commotion of Do What and Smokey running, they jumped to their feet.

Out of breath, Do What and Smokey collapsed in front of the log, resting their hands on their knees as if they just finished a sprint at the Olympic trials.

"Hey, fellas," Sam said. "You all look like you seen a ghost."

They explained with bated breath what had happened with Jacob and Peter leaving, the discovery of the dog, and finally escaping just in the nick of time. Do What told them about the gunfire, the booby trap, and Jacob falling into the pit. The brothers decided they had better get out of there before Peter and Jacob started after them.

Smokey thought about explaining other details of the congressman but he figured it wasn't the right time. They needed to get out of there before they were spotted.

From beyond the brush and trees, they could hear what sounded like footsteps running toward them.

They started to run; they didn't want to be caught or shot at. They didn't even look back to see that Ruby had emerged from the trees.

Smokey, who was in the rear, got tripped by the puppy. The puppy jumped on him, and Smokey yelped as she started to lick his face. The boys turned back and saw Smokey wrestling Ruby from his face as she licked him with a vengeance.

"Well, would you look at that," Larry said. "That puppy has found its mama."

They all laughed—besides Smokey, who was unsuccessfully struggling to stand up. He knew that if the puppy had caught up with him, Peter and Jacob wouldn't be far behind. They had to get out of there quickly.

Smokey got back up and motioned for the dog to go back.

"Get!" Smokey barked. But the dog only followed closer. The boys wanted to run, but the dog kept following. There was no way to get the dog to go back to the sack that had held her. She was attached to Smokey, her rescuer, and she wasn't going to let him go easily. If they waited around any longer, they would surely be found out. No amount of shooing or chasing Ruby away would keep her from following them.

"So, what are we gonna do with it?" Do What called to Smokey.

"I dunno," Smokey said. He had his shoulder bags from his paper route still around his shoulders. He bent and grabbed Ruby and stuffed her into one of the bags.

"What are you doing, Smokey? You gonna take their dog?" Bob asked.

"If I don't take her with us, she will give us away," Smokey said. They all began to run again. The puppy poked her head out, watching the trees go by as the boys made it back to town. Then he would figure out what to do with Ruby.

When the boys made it back to Cinder Bottom, they were out of breath and tired. They tried to compose themselves, but Bob, who was the heaviest of them all, was ready to pass out. Sam grabbed him by the arm and told him to keep going until they were out of sight. They stopped behind Lorenzo's place, trying to figure out what to do next. Thankfully, none of them had been spotted by Peter or Jacob, because the dog was a sure giveaway.

Smokey wasn't certain what to do with the puppy. He only knew that he needed to keep her away from Jacob and Peter. They had to find a place to keep her.

Smokey went down the line of brothers to see who could keep Ruby at their house.

"Don't look at me," Larry said.

Sam also shook his head.

Bob pointed to Larry. "What he said!"

Smokey knew better than to ask Do What. He had once had a much-loved dog, but his father had kicked it in a fit of rage. It had run away into the woods. Do What had never gotten over it, and though he loved dogs, he had no chance of bringing one home.

Smokey knew that it would be near impossible for him to bring a dog home himself. He had brought home strays before—stray dogs, kittens, and even a goat. His father never really cared, but his mother refused to have any more animals around. She said it was like having another child and that she had enough mouths to feed.

By this time, Ruby was starting to whine. Smokey worried that the crying puppy and big group of boys might start to draw attention, so the brothers decided to split up. Smokey and Do What took Ruby one way while the rest of the brothers went another.

Smokey instructed the brothers to cover for him. If anyone asked, they should say Smokey and Do What were walking up the railroad tracks to head to a fishing hole not far up the river. Smokey knew he'd be in trouble if word got back to his parents he was on the train tracks, but it would be a good alibi since there were virtually no people up there. His father constantly told him to stay off the tracks, and would remind him about Gladys, an older woman who had been killed walking on the tracks not too long ago.

Smokey tended to be the kind of kid that acted before he thought, and it would get him in a lot of trouble, even more so than other kids. Once, he and his brother had been in the woodshed, cutting wood with a hatchet. Smokey grabbed the hatchet, but his brother wanted it back. His brother reached out to take his branch. Without thinking, Smokey swung the hatchet and down it came, cutting off the end of his brother's thumb. His brother had yelped in agony as blood went everywhere. Though they searched, they never were able to find the tip of his thumb. Their parents took his injured brother to the doctor to get it taken care of.

Smokey had only been five years old, but his impulse to act had always been a bit ahead of his thinking. As he and Do What walked away with Ruby, he couldn't help but think that this was just another one of those times. This was serious; if Peter and Jacob were willing to protect the dog with rifles, there must be a reason, and they would be looking for her in town soon.

Ruby was whimpering again. Do What remembered that he had a small piece of beef jerky in his pocket. He reached down into the bag, and she devoured the small piece of dried meat.

They continued on their way, but knew they couldn't go home. They decided to head to the miner's house instead. If they could keep Ruby there for a bit, at least they would be out of sight, and they might be able to think about what to do next.

They made their way out of Cinder toward their hideout. When they passed by the ball field, they were lucky there was no one playing ball, and they let Ruby relieve herself. They quickly put her back into Smokey's shoulder bag and headed to the miner's house.

Do What bent over to lift Smokey up to unlatch the window and then open the door. Do What held Ruby in place on the ground with a foot on the end of the bag. With the window unlatched, Smokey climbed inside.

On his way to the door, he noticed a folding chair sitting in the middle of the floor. He was certain that they had put everything back the last time they were here. He let Do What and Ruby inside and pointed to the chair.

"Do What, didn't we put all the chairs back when we left the other night?" Smokey asked.

"Yeah, we did put them away. You think someone has been here?" Do What asked. They knew that they often shared this old house with a few other gangs, but since school started it was just the brothers that came on Friday nights after baseball. Who was in the house and what were they doing with a single chair in the center of the house?

There were many questions floating in Smokey's head, but the important one was what were they going to do with Ruby? Peter and Jacob were certainly searching. If they were supposed to have a secret, they couldn't very well go around asking people if they had seen a young black puppy wandering around. He couldn't stop wondering why this puppy, Ruby, was so valuable to them. Who was it for?

While Smokey contemplated these questions, Do What sat on the floor playing with Ruby. He was in his element, for a guy who really didn't open up much around people. He was like a dog whisperer. She followed him around and listened to his commands, sit and stay, like she was well-trained and ready. Do What had a special way with animals and children. There was something simple about his demeanor and his gentle spirit.

Smokey tended to get animals all worked up rather than calmed down, and he was grateful that Do What was there. He hadn't stopped to thank Do What for rescuing him at the moonshine still. He was amazed at how Do What always seemed to be at the right place at the right time. He never asked for any recognition. Smokey often took Do What for granted, but today he wanted to let him know he appreciated it.

"Do What, thanks for getting me out of that mess," Smokey said.

"You'd do it for me, Smoke," Do What replied.

They had been friends since the fourth grade when Smokey stole his lunch. Smokey was the kind of kid that saw an opportunity and he would take it. Looking back on it, Smokey felt bad for impulsively taking his lunch. Do What, with his good nature, had come after Smokey. Do What didn't try to take his lunch back at all. In fact, he offered to give Smokey his milk to boot. Smokey had stood, stunned, but took the milk anyway. From that day on, Do What tried to give Smokey his lunch.

One day, Smokey stopped him and asked him why he kept giving him his lunch. Do What said to him matter-of-factly, "I figured you don't have any food, so I wanted to share." That's when Do What became family. He had done nothing to deserve his generosity, and from that day forward, Smokey no longer tried to take his lunch. Instead, wherever he went, Do What followed. It has been that way ever since. Smokey turned to Do What, still on the floor with Ruby licking his face.

"Do What, we gotta figure out what to do," Smokey said.

Do What didn't say a word. He just saluted, their signal that all was well.

Do What often gave Smokey the "all is well" signal when he wasn't able to express in words what he meant, but they both knew what the salute meant. The salute meant that it would all work out and everything is as it should be.

Smokey always appreciated Do What's optimism, but this was a different kind of problem. It wasn't the same as when they had stole a few pieces of licorice from the Five and Dime in Bluefield. This problem was much bigger and much more complicated. It involved congressmen, agents, rifles, and now a stolen dog. They needed to figure out what the connection to Peter and the dog was or they wouldn't be able to figure out what to do. Ruby was having fun now, but she would need food, water, and a place to rest before too long. Smokey was determined to figure out what this whole dog situation was about.

Smokey figured his best bet would be to find out what Lorenzo knew about Peter. The situation was getting dire, and he needed answers now. Smokey decided to leave Ruby with Do What and go to town. He could get some sort of food for Ruby and go to Lorenzo to ask what he knew about Peter. If the congressman was now not a missing person and had gone back to Washington, then why was Peter, his aide, still in Cinder Bottom?

He said goodbye to Ruby and Do What and headed back to town. He knew that Lorenzo took lunch soon, which would give him just enough time to catch him before he left.

CHAPTER
8

Smokey wanted to be certain that he wasn't seen coming or going from the house. He left out the back window, the same one they used to go in and out.

He instructed Do What to create a makeshift leash. He could take some of the twine that he had used to hold one of the chair legs together. That way he could walk Ruby out back if she needed to relieve herself and not take a chance of letting her slip away.

Smokey felt a little bad to leave Do What alone, but he had to get to Lorenzo before he left for lunch. He tried to walk but found himself running and walking, stopping and going. He wasn't sure how else he could bring up the subject, so he contemplated just asking directly.

Smokey didn't know if dragging Lorenzo into this mess was a good idea, so he would just try to assess the situation once he got to his place.

When he arrived, Smokey was a bit sweaty and out of breath. He took a minute before walking in so that his breathing was slowed and he wiped the sweat from his brow. He looked toward Room 8 to see if there was any sign of Peter, but there was none. His car was gone too, which was a relief because he didn't know if he was ready to confront him yet. He was certain that he had not been spotted at the still.

Smokey took a deep breath and entered the office.

Signore Lorenzo was coming from behind the desk to lock the door and put the "out to lunch" sign in the window.

"Oh, Smokey, back again? Good to see you. I was just locking up for lunch," Lorenzo said. He ushered Smokey in, then hung the sign in the window, and prepared to lock the door. "You can stay a minute if you wish," he said. "I'm leaving a bit early; I have a package to pick up during my lunch today."

"I'll stay for a minute," Smokey said. He walked up to the counter and sat on the chair by the desk.

"What are you up to? Did you eat?" Lorenzo asked.

Smokey had forgotten about lunch and the idea of food was not appealing to him at that moment. But he would need to find something to bring back for Do What and Ruby.

"Not yet," he said.

"I could get you something if you want. You can watch the office, can't you? I was expecting someone and that's why I was getting lunch early and I don't want to miss them," Lorenzo said.

"Aww, sure I can watch the office," Smokey said. He was a bit hesitant because now he would have to wait to speak to him about Peter.

Lorenzo thanked him and turned the sign around on the window, placed his hat on his head, and left.

Smokey still wasn't sure how to get Lorenzo to tell him about Peter without tipping him off that he was fishing for information. He looked around on Lorenzo's desk to see if there were any clues about Peter. Taped on the top of his lamp was a message that said, "Tell Peter 'I am coming for the package today.'" There was no name after that. Could the package be the sack that Ruby was hiding in? Had Peter planned on bringing it here? Why would he hide out at the moonshine still if he was meeting someone at the boarding house?

Smokey lifted some papers and opened the desk drawer to see if there were any other clues about the meeting. There were no notes, but there was a small envelope. On the front of the envelope, it read, "For Mr. Brown." Smokey remembered that Peter was using a fake name at the boarding house and that Mr. Brown was the name he used.

He flipped the envelope over and read in bold words along the flap where it was sealed, "Do *not* deliver until after the exchange."

Smokey had to know what was in the envelope. He tried to open it gently to see if he could get a peek inside, but it was sealed tightly. Any pull would have torn the envelope. He remembered that Lorenzo kept a thermos for his afternoon coffee. Perhaps there was enough steam in it to open the envelope.

He looked beneath the desk and found the thermos. He placed it on the desk and opened it slowly. He saw a small plume of steam and grabbed the lip of the envelope to try to open it without tearing it. The steam began to release the glue and the flap started to lift open.

The bell for the office door sounded, and Smokey jumped. He quickly put the envelope in the drawer and placed the lid on the thermos.

It was a man that he didn't recognize. He was tall, handsome, and clean cut, like he just stepped out of a men's fashion catalog. He wore a white button-down shirt with a blue striped tie. He seemed too friendly to be a cop or a Fed, but Smokey was cautious.

Smokey stood to greet the gentleman.

"Good afternoon, sir," Smokey said with all his best schoolboy charm. "Can I help you?"

The man removed his hat and stepped closer to the desk. "Yes, you can help me. I'm looking to see if there is a note left for me."

"Are you a guest, sir?" Smokey asked, as if it was a normal procedure.

"No, I'm not, but I was told to come here for a message," the man said. The man seemed a bit nervous now, like he worried he may have the wrong place or information.

"What's your name, sir?" Smokey asked.

"My name is Peter Rose," he said.

Smokey tried not to stammer when he replied, but hearing that name to this face caught him off guard. He wasn't sure what to make of this.

"Sir, I can let Mr. Lorenzo know that you came by. If there's a message for you, Lorenzo will help you with that. He will return from lunch soon," Smokey said.

"That would be great. Tell him I will stop by again after a while. Thank you," the man said. He placed his hat on his head and walked out of the office.

Smokey stared after him through the window as far as he could see, but didn't know if he got into a car or just kept walking across the street. If this man was actually Peter Rose, then who was the other man that he had been calling Peter? He had seen an identity card in that other man's wallet that read Peter Rose. He realized that the man who had just presented himself as Peter Rose did not match up. When he and Do What had swiped that wallet back at Geneva's he was certain the photo matched the face of the guest in Room 8.

Could this man really be Peter Rose? If so, who was this Mr. Brown who was pretending to be him?

Smokey started to look for the details about the guest in Room 8. On the ledger it read, "Mr. Arnold Brown in Room 8," two times in the last week. He was gone for one night then returned the next day. His address was the same one in Bethesda, Maryland, that was on Peter's identification.

Smokey looked inside the box labeled Room 8 to see if there were any messages or notes for him. There was a note that read, "Don't forget our dinner plans at 7:00 p.m. tonight." There wasn't a signature or name on the note; the outside just had the number 8 written on it. If that was tonight, Smokey hoped he could find out where they were meeting and then figure out what they were meeting about.

Smokey remembered the envelope that had Mr. Brown's name on it and grabbed the thermos again to steam the envelope open. He opened the thermos and the steam quickly released the glue. He was able to lift the flap far enough to see that the envelope was filled with money—lots of it.

Smokey looked up to make sure he wasn't being watched. He steamed it open more to see if there was a note. Just in that moment, he spotted Lorenzo strolling across the front parking space. Smokey used the steam to reseal the envelope, place it back in the drawer, close the thermos, and set it back in its proper spot just in time.

The door flew open, and Lorenzo walked in with a small brown sack.

"Sandwiches," Lorenzo declared. He placed them on the counter and hung up his hat.

Smokey came out from behind the desk and sat in the chair in front of it. Lorenzo took out the sandwiches and gave one to Smokey and gestured for him to eat. He wasn't in the mood to eat; in fact, his stomach was turning a little. He thanked Lorenzo and began to take a few bites.

He waited until Lorenzo was nearly finished before he asked him about Room 8.

"Lorenzo, the man in Room 8 . . . what's his name, Mr. Brown, was it?" Smokey said. He took a small bite of his sandwich, waiting for him to reply.

"Yes, what about him?" Lorenzo asked, wiping the mustard from the corner of his mouth. "Did he stop by here while I was out?"

"No. But, a man I never saw before came and asked me if there was a message for him. I think he said his name was Mr. Rose," Smokey said.

Lorenzo stood up from his chair to pour a cup of coffee. He grabbed the thermos and offered Smokey a cup. He nodded yes and took one last bite of his sandwich. He wanted to save the other half for Do What. He wrapped half of the sandwich in the paper that Lorenzo handed to him. Lorenzo handed him a cup of coffee, and Smokey drank in small sips, waiting for the right words to emerge. He watched for Lorenzo's reaction, trying to gauge what the man might know.

"That's good that he came by. I had a message for him. I'm sure he'll return," Lorenzo said. They continued to sip coffee. Smokey shifted in his seat and leaned in toward Lorenzo.

"I'm sorry I didn't know there was a message for him or I would have given it to him," Smokey said. He pretended to be oblivious so his questions wouldn't be scrutinized. "Is Mr. Rose here for a long time, because I could deliver the message to him if it is urgent," he continued. Lorenzo grabbed the note from the lamp, balled it into a small wad, and tossed it in the rubbish bin.

"No, that's not necessary," Lorenzo said. He leaned back in his chair as if to savor the moment. "So many people come here Smokey, with their ideas about what this small town is about, but you and I know what it really is, don't we?" he said.

Smokey had a puzzled look on his face and asked, "What's that?"

"They all come here to be anonymous. To go unseen or unknown," Lorenzo declared. Smokey couldn't argue with that.

Smokey still couldn't figure out what to make of the agent, the congressman, his aide, and the missing dog. Why were they there and what was this whole incident really about? And who would care so much about a dog anyway? Though Ruby was sweet, she hardly seemed special in any way. Why would two people be willing to defend her with rifles? There had to be more to why they were there. Smokey tried to pry a bit deeper.

"What do you think Mr. Brown and Mr. Rose are trying to hide from here?" Smokey asked. He tried to act nonchalant about his statement but wasn't sure how Lorenzo might respond. Lorenzo sat back in his chair before answering. He took a deep breath.

"They're hiding from the life they have to live because they can't live the life they want," Lorenzo said matter-of-factly. "Take Mr. Brown for instance. He's been here several times. He never stays too long, he leaves late at night, he doesn't seem to know anyone or go to the beer joints or the houses like most men. He's here to do the bidding of someone else. He's here to be anonymous for someone else. He doesn't want to draw attention to himself."

"What about Peter Rose?" Smokey asked.

"He's here to find something, something that he has lost," Lorenzo said.

"Do you mean he physically lost something?" Smokey asked. He wasn't sure if Lorenzo was talking about Peter losing himself, like someone might lose his soul or his drive or ambition or if Lorenzo meant it more literally.

Lorenzo gazed up and placed his hands behind his chair. He leaned back a bit to contemplate his ideas. It was as if Smokey wasn't there, and he was contemplating these ideas alone. He had nothing but time on his hands some days, and they were filled with wondering and guessing about the mysterious lives of the people that came to Cinder Bottom.

Smokey was growing a bit impatient; he hadn't learned anything new except that Mr. Brown knew Mr. Rose. But who was the real Peter Rose? What were they hiding and what did Mr. Brown, if that was his name, want with a puppy? He had to return to the boarding house eventually, but what might he learn? How would he figure out what to do with Ruby? He was feeling a little anxious to return to Do What and Ruby with the sandwich and hopefully some useful information. So far he had nothing more than a sandwich.

Smokey remembered the note that Lorenzo threw away: *"Tell Peter 'I am coming for the package today.'"* Who was that note for? Was that for Mr. Brown, or was that message actually for the Peter Rose that Smokey met just a few minutes before? Perhaps the note had been referring to Ruby. Once it was discovered that there was no Ruby, there would be a problem. He had to think fast if he was going to get more information from Lorenzo.

"Lorenzo, a few days ago a man in a fancy car with D.C. plates asked me if I had seen anyone unusual. Did he come by here asking the same thing?" Smokey asked. He knew that if Lorenzo could give him at least a little more information he might pick up the scent of the trail that seemed to have gone cold.

Lorenzo stared at Smokey for what seemed like a very long time before answering. Maybe he was contemplating if he should tell him, or perhaps he sensed that Smokey was digging for information and wondered if he should say anything further.

"Yes, there was a man here in a fancy car, some big agent from Washington," Lorenzo finally said. "He was here yesterday asking questions." Lorenzo shifted in his seat and sat upright. He seemed genuinely interested in Smokey's question, as if he had been trying to piece things together as well. He didn't seem to mind the line of questions.

The chimes on the office door clanged. It was Peter again. He was even more handsome than Smokey had remembered when he stopped by just a few minutes earlier. He seemed poised and confident. He removed his hat and made his way to the desk.

Lorenzo rose to his feet.

"Mr. Lorenzo, good to see you today. I'm here to see if Mr. Brown has come by to collect my envelope that I left him," Peter Rose said.

"No, sir, not yet," Lorenzo said.

"Well, I'm sure he will be by soon. If you don't mind, I will just stop by again to see if he has left a message," Peter said. He tipped his hat as he placed it on his head and thanked Lorenzo for his kind help. Lorenzo waited until he had been gone for several seconds before turning to Smokey.

"That is a nice man, that Mr. Rose," Lorenzo said. "He gave me a two-dollar tip last time he was here. He is one classy gentleman."

Smokey thought he was an impressive man as well but wasn't sure if he had figured out if Lorenzo knew anything else about him.

"He's been waiting for Mr. Brown all day and hasn't been able to find him, which I think is strange in such a small town," Lorenzo said.

Smokey was getting impatient and wanted to know what the agent had said to him.

"So, about this agent, who was he looking for?" Smokey asked.

Lorenzo looked out the window as if he was being watched and said to Smokey, "I don't know. But, he kept talking about a girl named Ruby."

At this, Smokey's heart leapt. Could he have been looking for Ruby the dog? Was it not a girl he was looking for but a dog? Why would a federal agent care about a dog? This was getting to be more confusing by the moment, and he seemed to be digging himself into a deeper hole the more he asked questions.

"A girl?" Smoke said. "Who's Ruby?"

"He didn't say, which struck me as odd since he came such a long way," Lorenzo said, scratching his head, also perplexed.

Smokey had thought the agent was looking for a man, so why did he mention a girl named Ruby to Lorenzo? Smokey needed more information about the agent. He figured that Lorenzo could fill him in on the details about Mr. Brown and Peter, but he needed to know more about this girl. He wondered if he should speak to Ray next. If it was a girl and not a dog, he wanted to know who she was and why there was a dog with the same name.

He thanked Lorenzo for the sandwich and said he might stop by later to say hi before he headed home. He quickly ducked out the door and made sure that Mr. Brown was not lurking about waiting to seize him and take him away to some room for interrogation about the missing dog.

Once he saw the coast was clear, he headed to Ray's, the sandwich for Do What tucked into his shirt pocket. If he was going to figure out who the agent was looking for, he had to get to Ray before he left for the day. Ray often left early on Sunday so he could rest up for the week. He didn't really have any days off but would go play cards on Sundays at Big Ma's, and that was a perfect afternoon in his opinion.

Smokey suspected the agent might have the key to who this girl is and why they were hiding a dog named Ruby. His head was still spinning about the fact that the man he thought was Peter, might not be who he thought he was. If Peter Rose was the actual aide to the congressman who was missing, why was he in Cinder Bottom looking for Mr. Brown?

####

Smokey arrived at Raymond's grocery store to find Ray loading up his truck with some groceries for Big Ma. Smokey was a little out of breath, but he offered to help Ray finish loading up. Ray accepted and passed boxes and bags to him.

When the truck was loaded, Ray started to make his way around to the driver's side door, and Smokey ran to cut him off. He thought this might be his only chance to get the details about what the agent asked him about. He caught Ray off guard when he stepped in front of him.

"Ray, I have a question I wanna ask you," Smokey said.

Ray looked at him with his head cocked to the side.

"Yes, Smokey?" Ray prompted, looking at him intently.

"The other day, a nicely dressed man with city clothes came by here and was talking to you," Smokey began.

"Yes, he did," Ray replied slowly, not changing his disposition.

"Well, he stopped me too and asked me if I had seen anyone that seemed like they weren't from around here. I told him that most people in Cinder ain't from 'round here. But he didn't say who he was looking for. Did he tell you?" Smokey said, and then held his breath, waiting for Ray's response.

Ray opened the driver's side door and placed the last of the groceries for Big Ma inside, a special treat from the best bakery in Bluefield. He knew that Ma loved that place and he loved to surprise her.

"Smokey, he spoke to you as well? Why did he stop you?" Ray asked, sort of shocked.

Smokey told him about the "man" he was looking for, but never mentioned a name. He wanted to tell Ray the truth about the whole thing, the congressman's aid Peter Rose, the mysterious Mr. Brown, the moonshine still, and Ruby. He knew that he couldn't, though. He didn't want to get him involved. He was too deep in it now, but everyone else was just being questioned. He could be into something much more serious.

"He sure did make it seem important, and official," Smokey said. He was hoping that Ray would give some information in return and waited for some sign that he was willing.

"Now, he didn't ask about no man, though he did ask about a woman who might have come to find herself lost here in Cinder Bottom." Though Smokey was fourteen he knew what Ray meant by finding herself lost. He meant that sometimes, like Big Ma, girls flee from one place that is a bad situation to live here where everyone is anonymous. Those girls often end up as workers in the laundry, as a house helper, as a nannie, or in one of the houses if she was pretty enough to meet Big Ma's standards or one of the other houses run in Cinder.

"Did he say what she looked like?" Smokey asked. He knew he was now on cautious ground. He didn't want Ray to suspect he knew more than he did.

"No, he didn't say. He did mention she was a pretty young woman, but I told him I ain't seen no young lady 'round here," Ray said with a gentle drawl.

Smokey was busy processing the entire cast that was now involved with this unusual small-town drama: There was the agent, with the fancy Thunderbird from D.C., who was asking around about different people. Then there was the mysterious Mr. Brown from Bethesda, Maryland (or wherever he was really from), posing as Peter Rose. Mr. Rose was the aide to the once missing junior congressman. Then there was the man who claimed to be Peter Rose looking for Mr. Brown. There was also the Farmer boy who was with Mr. Brown at the still, and Ruby, a puppy who was apparently worth more than the boy's entire family.

Smokey could barely keep it all straight in his head. He wondered not for the first time how he got himself into these situations.

He thanked Ray, who was eager to leave. Ray drove off, leaving Smokey still a bit lost about what his next move was going to be.

He'd almost forgotten that Do What was with Ruby at the abandoned house, and he instinctively reached for his pocket where he placed the sandwich he saved for him. Smokey decided he needed to head back to relieve Do What and to make sure that he had at least something to eat. He figured he could give Ruby some of the bread crust to hold her over.

He made his way down the side streets to avoid the Farmer boy and Mr. Brown, just in case they did suspect him. He was certain that he wasn't seen but didn't want to take any chances.

He ran down back roads and alleys to finally make his way out of Cinder and toward Northfork and the abandoned house. He remembered that if he walked the railroad tracks, he would cut his time by ten minutes. He stopped on the tracks, looked both ways, and listened to see if he could hear the train. He was pretty certain that the train didn't run in the mornings on Sunday, which meant that it would go in the afternoon sometime.

Since he hadn't been paying attention, he hadn't noticed if the train had passed by yet. He knew that there was one spot that he would not be able to jump from the tracks and land safely. If a train came, he would be hit for sure.

He looked again and decided to chance it. He jumped over railroad ties, trying to move as quickly as he could to avoid the train. He was nearly there, and he could feel beads of sweat form on his brow, not from the heat but from the nervousness. He couldn't stop thinking about the old woman that his father told him about who was killed on the tracks. He tried to shake the thought from his mind and kept running.

The closer he got to the safe exit of the tracks, the harder he began to breathe. He was now sprinting, though one misstep would have caused him to fall.

Finally, the break in the brush was there and he leapt from the tracks to safety and continued to run toward the abandoned house.

He was out of breath when he arrived and went to the back window to call Do What. He called for him in a hushed voice to get him to come to the window.

"Do What!" he whispered. He paused, but there was no reply. He raised his voice and tried again. "Do What, can you hear me?" Smokey called.

There was no answer, and Smokey was growing impatient. He looked around for something to step on and found an old stump that he rolled to the window. It was just high enough for him to jump up to the edge of the window and pull himself in. He fell out of the window and onto the kitchen floor.

He jumped up and headed to the living room to tell Do What all about what he found out. When he got there, the chair was there leaning to one side.

Upon examination Smokey could see that the piece of twine used to hold it up was missing. There was no sign of Do What or Ruby.

Smokey called, "Do What, are you here?"

There was no reply. He peeked in the other room and the bathroom but there was no sign of them anywhere.

He must have taken Ruby out to relieve herself, he thought, and he walked toward the door. It was slightly ajar, which he figured Do What did on purpose so he wouldn't have to sneak back into the house with Ruby at the back window.

For a moment he was irritated because he could be spotted if he left by the front door, but after falling in the window, he didn't blame him for using the door, especially with a puppy in his hands.

He opened the door slightly to peek out. There was no sign of them, and he wondered if he should look for them rather than just wait. But he didn't figure they would be gone long.

Ten minutes passed. Do What hadn't returned, and Smokey knew that he shouldn't have been gone this long.

He peeked out the door and saw the Farmer boy from the still and Mr. Brown walking toward the abandoned house.

Smokey quickly shut the door and headed to the back window to go out the same way he came in. He was halfway out when the door slowly crept open.

The Farmer boy and Mr. Brown stepped in just as Smokey dropped out of sight. He sat under the eave to listen.

"The door is almost never unlocked, but it's empty, which is good. The brothers use this place once a week on Fridays, and it's empty the rest of the week. We should be fine here."

"You sure no one uses this place?" Mr. Brown asked.

"Naw, we have it all to ourselves," the boy said.

Mr. Brown peeked down the hallway and into the kitchen to make sure the coast was clear. "We gotta find that dog."

Smokey thought that Do What could return any minute through the front door with Ruby. He had to find a way to warn them before it was too late. He crept around the side of the house, hoping to find Do What and Ruby before Mr. Brown and the Farmer boy did. He didn't want to know what they might do to him if he showed up with the dog.

Right as he reached the front of the house, he saw Do What disappear through the front door with Ruby in tow. Smokey tried to motion for them to stop, but it was too late. The door was shut behind him.

Smokey made his way back to the window and on the log so he could try to hear their conversation. He didn't see the rifles with them when they walked in, which was good, but they may have a revolver hidden in the waist of their trousers.

Smokey crouched on the stump to stand just tall enough to catch what was being said.

"I said sit down," Mr. Brown ordered, speaking directly to Do What.

Do What pointed and protested. He still had the makeshift leash made from the twine on the chair in his hand, but the Farmer boy had picked up Ruby, who was squirming to get loose.

"Sir, that chair . . ." Do What said, pointing to the leg of the chair.

"Shut up and sit *down*," Mr. Brown said. Do What didn't argue, turned around, and sat on the chair, which collapsed immediately. Jacob laughed, and Ruby wiggled loose, ran to Do What, and immediately started to lick his humiliated face.

"Get up!" Mr. Brown howled.

Do What sat up and slowly made it up onto his feet, picking Ruby up again.

For a moment, Do What thought about trying to make it to the door and run. But there wasn't enough room between Mr. Brown and the door. He thought he might have a chance if he headed to the train tracks, but that would be risky especially with Ruby.

Do What stood, holding Ruby, and waited for his next instructions.

The man stood close to Do What's face, inspecting his eyes. "Where did you get the dog?" Mr. Brown asked.

"I found her," Do What said, which, in fact, wasn't entirely false. "She started following me, and I just picked her up."

Mr. Brown stared into his eyes to search for any deception. Spotting none, he snatched Ruby from Do What's arms and handed the puppy back to Jacob without looking.

"So why are you here?" Mr. Brown said, watching Do What with careful eyes.

"Same as you, I guess. Just hiding out," Do What said with perfect innocence.

"We ain't hiding, are we, boy?" Mr. Brown said.

The Farmer boy looked at him and was going to contradict the man but figured he ought to keep his mouth shut. He was already in trouble for losing Ruby in the first place.

Jacob shook his head to indicate that they were not hiding, though technically they were. But why hide? Who were they hiding from? Peter Rose, perhaps. What was the money that was left for Mr. Brown in Lorenzo's desk? Did that have something to do with it?

Questions raced through Smokey's mind as he listened from beneath the kitchen window. He hoped that Do What would cooperate and not do anything stupid to upset Mr. Brown. He knew that he would be fine as long as they didn't try to harm Ruby. He was certain that since the dog had some value they wouldn't do anything to harm her.

Ruby was again trying to wiggle free from Jacob. She whined and pulled to get away from him. The boy held her even tighter. He held her so tight that she turned and bit him hard, and he flung her across the room where she hit the wall and fell to the floor, whimpering.

"That hurt, you little flea bag!" Jacob yelled.

Not a moment passed before Do What jumped to Ruby's defense. He grabbed Jacob by his shirt collar and punched him square in the nose, knocking him down and bloodying his face.

Do What raced to get Ruby, but Mr. Brown stood between them. He pulled a revolver from his waist and aimed it at Do What.

"Stay right there." He turned to the Farmer boy and shouted for him to get up. He was angry because the boy had hurt the dog, but even more upset that the boy had escalated the situation.

Now Do What knew that something was going on beyond the missing dog.

Do What froze and stared at Ruby, who was whimpering on the floor. The gun was aimed right at him. He contemplated what he would do next. He wouldn't let them harm or take Ruby. He never bothered to ask Smokey why this whole situation was something that he cared about. He trusted Smokey. If he was interested, so was Do What. But now this went beyond his loyalty to Smokey—it was personal. They had caused Ruby harm.

He stepped forward to get Ruby, and Mr. Brown raised the gun, pointing it at Do What's face. Do What stopped and stared at the barrel of the revolver. He frowned, angrier than he was afraid.

Mr. Brown pointed the revolver to Jacob and told him to get the twine used to make Ruby's leash and tie Do What to the chair.

The Farmer boy made his way to Ruby and knelt to untie the leash. She turned her head and bit him again, this time drawing blood. He cried out in pain and raised his hand to hit her.

Mr. Brown turned to him before he could and said, "Don't you dare."

Do What smirked as if to say, "Good girl, Ruby."

Jacob removed the makeshift leash, and Mr. Brown gestured for Do What to move toward the chair. The Farmer boy propped the chair against the wall so it wouldn't fall and instructed Do What to sit down, then he tied Do What to the chair.

Smokey couldn't see what was happening but hoped that Do What was going along with whatever they told him to do. He couldn't just let his friend take the heat for the missing dog when it was his fault.

From the kitchen window, Smokey could see where Do What was tied to the chair leaning up against the wall. He wanted to get Do What's attention without being seen, but he would have to be careful. If they were both caught, there would be no chance to get away.

In this moment, Smokey wished that he could summon the sheriff and tell him everything he knew. He wished that he wasn't so curious and could have kept his friends out of this trouble, but it was too late for that.

He lifted himself up over the windowsill and tried to get Do What's attention without being seen by the other two. If Do What would just glance his way, he could signal to him. Once he almost made eye contact with Do What, but then Mr. Brown stepped close to the chair and waved the gun in Do What's face.

"Now, I know you didn't mean to get involved, son, but it's too late, you are. It sure was bad luck that you found this dog. It was lucky for us, but bad for you," Mr. Brown said. He paced back and forth and peeked at his watch. He was late to meet Mr. Rose and needed to go to the boarding house to meet him. He didn't want to take the boy with him. He needed to get Mr. Rose to come to the miner house and not draw any unwanted attention. He didn't want to risk having his plan fail.

He told the Farmer boy that he was going to leave him here with the dog and Do What, and that he was not supposed to do a thing, just watch and keep him tied up. The boy nodded and said he would be fine to watch them both. Mr. Brown left through the front door, and Smokey stayed out of sight until he was sure the man was gone.

Smokey stood on the log beneath the window so he could see Do What. When he rose, he saw him looking in disdain in the boy's direction. He turned and saw Smokey. His eyes widened in relief, and Smokey saluted him, the signal that all is well. Do What smiled to himself and turned away from the window back toward the boy.

Smokey got down off the log and made his way to the front door. He wanted to cause a distraction so he could draw the Farmer boy out of the house and then free Do What. He probably only had one shot to do this. He found a coal bucket just outside the porch along with a small shovel. He figured if he could cause enough of a ruckus, he could lure the boy out of the front door.

Inside, the Farmer boy had approached Ruby. He knelt down beside her, and she growled at him. He looked up at Do What and grabbed Ruby by the neck. He let her dangle by the flesh of her neck as he taunted Do What. She cried and tried to get away, but it was no use. The hairs on the back of Do What's neck stood up.

"Leave her alone," Do What said. His face turned a bright red and his nose flared with anger. The boy approached him, dangling the dog, who was now yelping.

"What are you gonna do about it?" Jacob said. He held Ruby right in Do What's face.

Do What's fists clenched and he pulled the twine that bound him taut on his wrists. The boy swung Ruby in front of his face as she whined. The blood in his veins boiled, and he could feel beads of sweat as they formed on his face. His breathing grew deeper with each breath.

Jacob smirked. He hadn't forgotten the bloody nose that Do What gave him.

He was now swinging Ruby in his face and teasing him to do something. Do What could not stand Ruby's whimpers any longer, nor could he stand the boy's taunting. Taking in a strong breath, Do What broke his hands free from the twine and bolted up from his seat.

The Farmer boy was caught off guard and held Ruby out in front of him as if to use her as a shield.

In that moment, Smokey opened the door, wielding a coal shovel. He swung at Jacob, hitting him in the head. His eyes rolled, and he dropped Ruby to the floor as he fell with a thud.

CHAPTER
9

"Hey, Smoke," Do What said. He leaned down to scoop the puppy off the floor, hugging her into his arms.

"Hey, Do What," Smokey said in return.

Do What saluted him.

They decided to tie Jacob up and leave him in the center of the floor. The Farmer boy was breathing just fine, and besides the lump on his head from getting knocked out, he would come to at any moment and be mad as all get-out.

They locked the front door and crawled out the window, just in case Mr. Brown was close to returning. Smokey climbed out of the window onto the log first. Do What then passed Ruby to him, and they stepped down to safety. Do What was so focused on passing down Ruby, he hadn't heard the footsteps behind him.

Jacob had woken up and somehow broken free from his restraints. He was pulling on Do What's leg. Do What flailed and kicked. One of those kicks landed the Farmer boy square in the face, and he fell to the ground, unconscious. Do What practically fell out the window on top of Smokey and Ruby.

They all tumbled to the ground. Ruby whimpered but then started to lick their faces. They jumped up, knowing they probably only had a few minutes before Mr. Brown was back or the boy came to.

They both knew the only way to avoid running into Mr. Brown and stay clear of the Farmer boy was to return to Cinder Bottom from Northfork on the railroad tracks. Neither Smokey nor Do What had heard the train's whistle, which meant that it still had to pass by on those tracks. They were running short on time, and each moment counted.

They ran up the trail that Smokey came from toward the entrance to the tracks, a small trail not visible from far away. Do What had Ruby tucked in his shirt so he could run. He was now in this for Ruby, and he was going to do whatever was necessary to keep her safe.

They were making good time running down the tracks though they knew they were just entering the blind spot that there was no place to run or jump from if a train came. The same spot where the old woman died that Smokey's dad had warned him about. They didn't have a choice. They had to run.

Do What tripped and nearly landed on top of Ruby, but both were fine. Smokey stopped and turned around to help him up. That's when he noticed the Farmer boy hobbling in the distance toward them.

Jacob was filled with rage, his face still covered in the dried blood from where he was punched by Do What. He had a shoe mark on his face from the kick he received from him as well.

"Get up, Do What, we gotta get outta here!" Smokey said. They sprang to their feet and made their way as fast they could go. The boy was injured so he couldn't follow very quickly. He was still a considerable distance away. They were entering the point of no return, the place where if a train came, they couldn't jump, dodge, or escape it.

They pressed on listening for even the faintest sound of the train. They were almost halfway through the blind spot when the train whistle sounded. They stared at each other in terror and continued to run.

They were nearly in a place where they could jump to safety on a small clearing away from the tracks. They raced ahead and leapt before looking back to see where the Farmer boy was. He was only halfway through the blind spot. The train whistle was blowing more fiercely now.

Smokey got up first and turned to Do What. "Let's go," he said.

Do What turned to Smokey and said, "What if he doesn't make it?"

Smokey paced once, then looked up the tracks to see how far he was from leaving the blind spot. The train was getting closer and the Farmer boy looked terrified, running as fast as he could. But then he tripped and fell on the tracks. His leg was wedged in between the tracks.

Smokey turned to Do What and then leapt to the tracks, running for the Farmer boy.

He felt insane headed directly to the exact spot where there is no way of escaping and a train barreling toward him. Smokey figured he probably deserved it for all the times he didn't get caught when he probably should have when he had done something that could have gotten him into trouble. But this was real trouble, the kind that could end your life.

When Smokey arrived, there were tears streaming down the boy's cheeks, and he was calling for Smokey to help him. Smokey reached down and turned the boy's foot so he could get up. They had only seconds to move or they would be killed. The instant that Smokey pulled Jacob's leg free, they ran. They ran faster than either of them had ever ran before, yelling the entire way. Do What, who was clinging to Ruby in the clearing, was crying for them to run faster.

The train was within a dozen yards, and they had seconds to make it to the clearing. The train would not be forgiving. It would not care that they never wanted this to happen.

The last and longest whistle sounded. They heard the screech of the train's breaks. The iron beast slowed just enough to allow the boys to leap into the air and land in the bushes just before the clearing as the train raced by.

Do What cheered. He stood up and searched for the boys. They were lost in the thicket of bushes. Their heaving breathing could be heard mixed with sighs and tears.

The next moment, Do What could hear laughter, uncontrollable laughter. Jacob and Smokey could not stop laughing. They were genuinely happy to be alive and nothing else in that moment mattered.

Do What looked at Smokey and saluted him.

Smokey gave him the bird and continued to laugh. They all did.

They weren't sure what to do next. Jacob reached out his hand and helped Smokey to his feet.

"Thanks for helping me," he said.

"Sure," Smokey said, dusting himself off.

They both made their way to the clearing and headed down the path back to the street. Neither of them talked for the first few minutes. There was so much adrenaline and yet the importance of what they were doing before seemed like it didn't really matter.

"I'm Do What," Do What said, holding his hand out to the boy.

The boy seemed reluctant since the only time that Do What had ever extended his hand out was to punch him. The boy placed his hand in his and shook it.

"Jacob," the boy said.

It was then that they realized that he was almost their age, maybe sixteen or seventeen. He had seemed so much older when he was dangling Ruby in front of his face.

"I'm Smokey," Smokey said, placing his hand out to shake as well.

They continued to walk to town and weren't certain where they were headed. They wondered if Mr. Brown had returned to the house and found Jacob, Do What, and the dog had all gone missing. He would certainly be driving back to Cinder Bottom by now if that was the case. They had to figure out what they were going to do.

"So why do you need the dog so bad?" Smokey said, looking at Jacob to watch his reaction.

"Mr. Brown actually stole the dog and was using it as leverage against Peter Rose, some big wig up north," Jacob said.

Finally, someone was making sense. Smokey now knew what the money was for in Mr. Lorenzo's drawer and why Peter Rose was looking for Mr. Brown: to get Ruby back.

"Where was the dog taken from?" Smokey asked.

"I guess it was taken from the veterinarian by Mr. Brown. He used a fake ID with Mr. Rose's identity,"

Jacob said. "Mr. Brown likes to talk and told me all the details, even though I don't care."

"Then why are you helping him?" Do What asked.

"He followed me up to the still one afternoon and told me that if I didn't help him, he would have the Feds there to take the still and arrest my dad. I didn't have a choice," Jacob said.

They were nearly in Cinder Bottom when Smokey said, "We can still get the dog to Mr. Rose and see if we can get Mr. Brown taken care of by Sheriff Donnie." They all liked the idea.

"But how do we find Peter Rose here in Cinder Bottom?" Do What asked.

"I know where he will be," Smokey said.

They headed to Lorenzo's, careful to watch the streets and keep an eye out for Mr. Brown.

The boys didn't want to be found before they located Peter Rose and the sheriff. They made their way behind Big Ma's and saw Ray on the porch playing cards as he always did on Sunday afternoon. He waved at the boys.

They waved back but hurried past without stopping. Do What had Ruby tucked in his shirt, but her squirming was making him jump and move in strange ways, and they didn't want to attract attention to themselves.

Once they passed Geneva's, they were nearly at the parking lot of Lorenzo's boarding house. There was no sign of Mr. Brown's car, but they wanted to be safe. They ducked behind the building while Smokey agreed to go in to see Lorenzo and find out if he had spoken to Peter Rose yet.

When he got inside, he found Lorenzo playing his opera records and dusting. Smokey couldn't figure why he liked all that yelling and yodeling. He really hated it but sat and listened to it sometimes with Lorenzo as he dusted just to keep him company. Lorenzo would describe the opera to him, explaining what was happening during each song. He would retell the Marriage of Figaro and how incredible the story was. Smokey found that the music was starting to grow on him. He appreciated that he could tell that there was a storyline, when before it sounded like a lady screaming for no reason. He didn't want to interrupt Lorenzo but the bell announced him to the room.

Lorenzo could always tell that it was Smokey, even if he didn't look. He said it was something about how Smokey opened the door that made sure he always knew it was him. When Smokey entered, Lorenzo held up his hand as if to say, "Don't say anything."

Smokey didn't interrupt; he just sat in the chair by the desk while the music moved to a crescendo, a word that Lorenzo taught him. When the piece was over, he sat on the desk next to Smokey.

"That opera always gets me," Lorenzo said. Then he stood and walked around to the other side of the desk. He looked at Smokey oddly, staring at him for an unusually long time. Smokey could sense Lorenzo knew something was going on. He shifted in his chair, not sure what to say.

"Nice song, Lorenzo," Smokey ventured.

"Now I *know* something is going on. You hate opera," Lorenzo said. He walked around to where Smokey was sitting. "Smokey, what's going on?" he asked.

Now there was no more escaping. Smokey was in a pinch. Perhaps Lorenzo was the man to help, but he didn't want to get him involved. He just wanted to know if Peter Rose had come by again.

"Wait right here." Lorenzo walked out the door.

Smokey knew this was his chance, so he walked around the desk to see if the envelope was still there for Mr. Brown. If neither Mr. Brown nor Mr. Rose had been there yet, there might still be time to get to the sheriff. But what would he tell him: that they took a dog and a man wants it back? They didn't have any evidence besides Jacob's word, which wasn't worth much in Cinder Bottom. They needed real proof that Mr. Brown had stolen the dog and was blackmailing Mr. Rose who was trying to get it back.

He opened the drawer and saw the envelope with Mr. Brown's name. It was still there. The bell rang and Lorenzo walked in. Smokey reached down and grabbed the thermos of coffee.

"Do you mind if I have some?" Smokey asked, reaching for a cup.

"No, go right ahead," Lorenzo said.

Smokey, relieved that Lorenzo hadn't seen him looking in his desk, poured himself a cup of coffee, still piping hot. He walked from behind the desk sipping from his cup. Lorenzo had something behind his back. He wasn't sharing what it was, but Smokey could see he was hiding something.

Lorenzo pulled his hand out from behind his back and dangled a leash and collar in front of Smokey's face. Smokey looked at him, puzzled.

"What's this for?" Smokey asked, staring at the leash in disbelief. He wondered how he knew he could use a leash.

"This is for Ruby," he said.

Smokey spat a bit of his coffee back into his cup.

"For Ruby?" he said, trying to act confused. He didn't know what to say.

Lorenzo held the leash straight out in front of him. Smokey stood there frozen like a statue. He realized he had to get with it fast or he would be found out. Smokey grabbed for the leash and pulled it and the dog collar to himself quickly. He knew he only had a few moments before Mr. Brown or Peter Rose showed up, so he took this chance to come clean.

"How did you know?" Smokey said.

"I knew you had the dog the moment you didn't eat the sandwich in your pocket," Lorenzo said.

Smokey reached for his pocket, and he could feel the mustard oozing through his shirt. With all the commotion he had forgotten he had it there. He wondered how half a sandwich would tip off Lorenzo that he had the dog. He wondered how he knew about the dog in the first place.

"How did you . . . ?" Smokey tried to ask a complete question but got lost in his thoughts. He was standing, facing Lorenzo, when the bell behind him sounded for the door.

Smokey quickly slid the leash and collar into his pants pocket. He was terrified to turn around. If it was Mr. Brown at the door, he would be done for. Smokey felt trapped and didn't want to look.

"Good afternoon, Signore Lorenzo," a voice said.

Smokey knew that voice. The familiar and proper way of speaking was distinctive, and Smokey turned when he was certain that it was Mr. Rose.

He watched as the men shared greetings and shook hands. They acted like they had known each other for years. After the two men exchanged some whispers, Mr. Rose left.

As soon as he was gone, Smokey spoke up quickly. "Lorenzo, that's Mr. Rose, the congressman's aide!" Smoke declared. He was still not sure how much he knew about Ruby and didn't want to tell him unless he already knew.

"Yes, it was," Lorenzo said and made his way back to his desk. He opened the drawer, slid something inside, and closed it quickly. He didn't mention what it was, but somehow Smokey knew it had something to do with Mr. Brown.

"I need you to do me a favor, Smokey," Lorenzo said, holding Smokey by the shoulders. "You need to go to Geneva's."

Smokey, of course, knew where Geneva's place was and would happily go, but why did Lorenzo want him to go? He thought for a second and then replied.

"Yes, of course."

"You need to give this to Geneva."

Lorenzo handed him an envelope, the same one with Mr. Brown's name on it from his desk, the one with the money. Lorenzo had a serious look on his face and placed the envelope into his hands.

Smokey was still confused. He was uneasy and now feeling more lost than ever. What would he tell Jacob and Do What? He still didn't know what to do with Ruby.

"Tell the boys to bring Ruby around back. They can keep her in my apartment until you return," Lorenzo said. "But you need to go now," he said, sternly.

"Okay," Smokey said. He'd known Lorenzo long enough to know that this was serious. He couldn't waste any time.

He grabbed the envelope and shoved it into his pocket. He headed out the door and ran directly to where the boys were hiding.

After handing the leash and collar to Do What, Smokey explained that Lorenzo would take them in. He told them where to meet him behind the building.

They looked uneasy but did as they were told.

"Where are you going?" Jacob asked. He didn't trust the orders, and while he would do just as he was told, he was still interested in where Smokey was going.

"I'm going to Geneva's. Stay out of sight, and I'll see you in a few," Smokey said. He turned and started down the alley to Geneva's.

The boys watched as he left, and then they headed up the alley to Lorenzo's apartment behind the boarding house.

Smokey had a feeling that there was more to his errand than just dropping off the envelope. Halfway there, he realized that Lorenzo didn't tell him anything, just that he should head to Geneva's and give her the envelope. He didn't delay, though. He figured it would all make sense or Lorenzo wouldn't have sent him there.

He was nearly there when he ran into Ray.

"Hey there, Smokey. Where are you going in such a hurry?" Ray asked.

"Sorry, Mr. Raymond. I'm headed to Geneva's," Smokey said. He was out of breath. He didn't know how to excuse himself, but he wanted to run. He started to edge around the man so he could continue.

"Settle down for a second. I'm here to help," Ray said. He stopped Smokey, held his shoulders the same way that Lorenzo did to get his attention, and made sure he could see his eyes.

Smokey paused and looked at Ray.

"Do you have something for me?" Ray asked.

Smokey was alarmed and didn't know what he was talking about. He had to get to Geneva's and didn't have time to play games with Ray. If he didn't get there, who knows what would happen. But he saw the kindness in Ray's eyes and finally stopped his hurried state.

Ray held out his hand. "I'll take the envelope Lorenzo gave you," he said.

Smokey reached into his back pocket and handed Ray the envelope without hesitating. Ray didn't even look at it; he just placed it into his back pocket.

"Now you need to go to Geneva's as planned," Ray instructed. "You'll need this." He handed Smokey another envelope. Unlike the one from Lorenzo's desk, this one was thin and blank without any words on the outside.

Ray looked at him with confidence. "Once you're done there, I want you to meet me at Big Ma's, you understand?" Ray asked.

Smokey nodded and then ran for Geneva's.

When he arrived, he almost gasped out loud at the sight of Mr. Brown sitting right there at the counter. He was in the exact same place where he and Do What first spotted him, with the same jacket draped over his chair. He was just getting up to go to the bathroom.

As soon as Mr. Brown was out of sight, Geneva walked right up behind Smokey, carrying a steaming pot of coffee.

"Did you bring it?" Geneva asked, startling him.

Smokey was not sure what she knew but didn't want to start a stammer of lies that he would have to back out of. Instead, he nodded and reached into his pocket. Smokey handed the envelope to Geneva without hesitation.

Geneva set the pot of coffee on the counter, ripped into the envelope, and read the note inside. She then crumpled it up and shoved it into her apron pocket without saying a word.

"You go on now and git yourself outta here before he comes back," Geneva said.

Smokey turned to leave. He glanced backward and saw Geneva pouring coffee into Mr. Brown's cup. Mr. Brown came back, and she smiled and engaged him in conversation. Smokey was more confused than ever: now Geneva was part of this? What was on that note in the envelope from Ray?

Smokey took off toward Big Ma's with his mind racing faster than his feet. Now Lorenzo, Ray, and Geneva were involved with this complicated puzzle. He wanted to stop to think, but he knew he had to get to Big Ma's. *What's her involvement?* Smokey wondered.

He made his way to the back alley that led to the back porch where Big Ma sat on Sundays when the card game was over.

Big Ma was sitting in her rocking chair, drinking her sweet tea, when Smokey rounded the corner of the porch. He was again out of breath but tried to collect himself before saying hello to Big Ma.

She motioned for him to join her on the porch in the empty rocker beside her. She had a glass of sweet tea waiting for him.

He sat next to her, still breathing like a racehorse.

"Sweet tea?" Big Ma said.

Smokey didn't answer but nodded and nearly guzzled his tea. He finished half the glass and stopped to breathe, setting the glass down on the small table between them.

Big Ma didn't flinch, she just continued to sip her tea and rock in her chair.

Smokey wasn't sure what to do next. He figured that Ray might show back up to tell him what to do. Big Ma gave no indication that she had any instructions for him, but she had seemed to be waiting with a glass of tea just for him. Big Ma liked cigars whenever Ray surprised her with one from Bluefield. She was smoking one now, and she took a long slow drag. She released a large puff of smoke and then grinned. There was nothing as simple and pleasurable to her as sitting, drinking her sweet tea, and enjoying her cigar.

Smokey's breathing returned to normal as he processed what just took place. He wished he had told the brothers what was happening. He had gotten them involved when they went to the still, and Smokey almost got shot. He wondered where they were and if they would forgive him for hiding this from them. They usually didn't keep any secrets. Smokey had done a few things that he kept to himself, but if it involved them, he always kept them informed.

He began to mimic the same pace as Big Ma and rocked back and forth in a gentle stride. He was so content being with Big Ma that his anxiousness to find Ray started to drift away. Being with Big Ma felt like everything would be okay. He felt that while he sat on that porch nothing could harm him. He knew that it wasn't true but wanted to sit with this for at least another moment. He remembered that Ray said he would meet him here at Big Ma's. At that moment, he had nothing he had to do, so he just rocked.

Ray arrived just a few minutes later. His truck bounced down the alley and parked right in front of the porch. He stepped out of the driver's seat and made his way up the stairs.

Smokey and Big Ma acknowledged his arrival but didn't stop rocking. She handed him a glass of sweet tea and then continued to rock. Ray knew better than to interrupt Big Ma and waited for her to speak.

"Afternoon, Ray," Big Ma said, signaling that it was fine to speak.

Ray took another sip on his tea before replying.

"Afternoon, Ma," he said. "Smokey, we need to go."

"Go where?" Smokey asked. Ray and Big Ma stared at him, making no other sound. He regretted asking the moment the words left his mouth. He stood and thanked Big Ma for the tea and followed Ray, who gulped down the rest of his tea.

"Here, you'll need this," Big Ma said, handing him the sack that Ruby had once been in.

He thanked her, took the sack, and followed Ray to the truck.

He got into the passenger's side of Ray's truck. He had never been inside it before. Ray had given him and Do What a ride once to Bluefield, but they sat back in the bed of the truck. Being in front felt like it was a big deal. When Ray started driving down the road, Smokey glanced at the sack that was in his hands. How did Big Ma get the sack? What would he need it for now?

Ray didn't say a word. He just headed toward Northfork. Maybe Ray was taking him home, to his house, to tell his parents all that he had been involved in. The whole shenanigan would be over in just a few more minutes now that Ray was driving. Smokey wanted to know how this complex puzzle fit together, but honestly, he was relieved that he was being turned into his parents by Ray.

I'll vow never to meddle in other people's business again, he thought. He might tell his parents that it was all just a misunderstanding, being in the wrong place at the wrong time, which was partially true. But he knew that he was the reason he and his friends were involved, and he would come clean when confronted.

They drove into Northfork, passed the baseball field, and then passed the turn off to the holler where Smokey lived.

"You passed the way to my house, Ray," Smokey spoke up.

"We aren't going to your house," Ray said.

They continued to drive, and they eventually pulled up to the back side of the abandoned miner's house. Smokey was confused. Why had Ray brought him here?

Ray turned to Smokey. "You need to wait here."

Smokey looked at Ray but didn't protest. He opened the door to the truck and stepped out. Ray handed him the sack.

"Stay out of sight back here behind the house," Ray said. "Smokey, I'm not playing. Don't move. Don't go nowhere and don't do nothing till I get back here, you got it?" Then he drove off down the road, not waiting to give any further instructions.

Smokey stayed out of sight but was uncertain what or whom he was waiting for. The dust sputtered behind the truck as it raced back down the road toward Cinder Bottom.

He had spent so much time trying to figure out the mystery of the missing congressman, the agent, Peter Rose, Ruby, and Mr. Brown but had no idea what might be next. He wondered what Do What and

Jacob were doing and how little Ruby was holding up. He wondered if Lorenzo told Ray about Peter Rose and that's how Big Ma knew. He wondered how long he would have to wait behind the house. What was he waiting for anyway?

He sat and remembered the other half of the sandwich. He peeked into his front pocket to find it smashed and oozing mustard. He thought that it was a waste of a perfectly good sandwich. He was hungry and wished he had eaten the rest when he had the chance. Now it was ruined, though he considered eating it anyway.

Smokey sat for a minute and thought of his quiet, peaceful time rocking on Big Ma's porch and how she never seemed bothered by much. He was not patient like her. He started to grow anxious the longer he waited. He had no idea what he was waiting for, and his impatience increased with each passing minute.

He could no longer stand just waiting for something to happen, so he stood and peeked around the house. He spotted Mr. Brown's car pulled up in front of the house.

He ducked down, waiting to see what he was doing there. Maybe he had returned to relieve Jacob of his post or find out what had happened to Do What and Ruby. Perhaps he still had no idea that they had escaped and Ruby wasn't there. Once he found out they were missing, he would certainly go looking for them in town.

Mr. Brown got out of the car and headed to the front door. Smokey snuck around the side of the house to see if he had entered already.

CHAPTER
10

When he made it to the front of the house, he was able to see that Mr. Brown had entered the front door and closed it behind him. Smokey figured it would be a matter of minutes before he came right back out when he discovered that Ruby and the boys were gone. He would probably yell and storm back to his car, cursing all the way. If Ruby was as valuable as Mr. Brown said she was, then he would be in a hurry to get her back.

Smokey waited for the burst of energy and the door to fling open any second, but the door never opened. He was a bit confused but waited out of sight just the same. If the man thought that the dog and boys were just outside, perhaps he might head back out around the house to search.

He positioned himself where he could keep an eye on the front door but be ready to run into the bushes toward the railroad tracks at a moment's notice. He was fortunate that Mr. Brown only knew him from times he was at Lorenzo's boarding house and had no idea he was involved. He was grateful that he didn't have Do What with him when he was there visiting with Lorenzo so he didn't make the connection that they might know each other.

Smokey was now feeling a bit uncertain because if he had already discovered that Do What, Jacob, and Ruby were gone, why was he waiting so long to come out of the house? What might he be doing? Was he hoping that they returned and he would be there waiting? What would he do if he found any of the boys? Would he try to cover his tracks?

Smokey remembered that Mr. Brown had a revolver tucked in his waist and worried that he would use force to get what he wanted. If Do What, who was by now attached to Ruby, refused to give her up, someone could get hurt. Smokey could never forgive himself if that person was Do What. He loved dogs and he would never let harm come to a dog again, not on his watch. Do What was the kind of person that was so loyal that the thought of leaving a dog to some unholy demise was not going to happen.

It had now been several minutes and there was no sign of Mr. Brown. Smokey went to the window that he crawled into before and stood up on a log to see if he could see or hear anything. He was careful not to make any noise and sat beneath the ledge for a minute, listening to see if he could hear anything.

He thought he heard the faint sound of voices, but he couldn't be certain. Who would Mr. Brown be talking to? Himself, perhaps?

Smokey sat in silence trying to hear anything else, but he heard nothing. Maybe his imagination was running wild, and he just thought he heard voices.

He decided to risk standing up tall on the log to see if he could see anyone. He knew that he could see part of the living room from the window, so he had to be careful because he didn't want to be caught. He got up slowly. The window was closed so it would be hard to hear anyone, but if he could get a glimpse inside, he could figure out what his next move would be.

He heard Ray's voice in his head: "Stay out of sight." But he needed to know why Mr. Brown wasn't leaving. He couldn't just sit behind the house and wait. *What am I waiting for anyway?* he thought.

When he looked through the window, he saw Mr. Brown was standing facing toward him. He immediately ducked back down. He waited a minute and then stood again. In the corner of the living room, he could see Do What tied to the chair with the twine that was Ruby's leash. Smokey gasped and cupped his hands over his mouth and ducked down in fear that he would be heard. He waited to be certain that he hadn't been discovered before he stood again.

He couldn't figure out how Do What was there already. If Mr. Brown had just arrived, how did Do What get here?

He stood again and saw Mr. Brown waving his hands at Do What. He pointed to the chair. Jacob stepped forward and started to untie Do What's hands with one hand while he held Ruby in the other.

What were they all doing there? He had left them at Lorenzo's. How did they get back to the house? Did Mr. Brown discover them at Lorenzo's? If so, why would they be back there? Nothing was making sense. He had to do something; this was the exact situation they had been in a few hours ago.

Then the thought crossed his mind that Jacob had turned on Do What and brought them back to save his own ass and family. Smokey boiled with anger at the thought. He couldn't believe he had rescued Jacob only to have him turn on all of them and bring them back to the house.

Smokey needed a plan to get them loose. He needed a distraction to get Mr. Brown and Jacob out of the house. If he got them out of the house, then he could sneak in and untie Do What and get Ruby out. But what would cause Mr. Brown to leave the house? He sat thinking when he heard some voices in the distance, outside the front of the house.

He peeked around the front of the house to see who it was. He saw Sam, Bob, and Larry headed to the miner house. He had to warn them to stay out and remain quiet or they could ruin everything. He wondered what they were doing. He hadn't seen them since this morning when they were hiding by the still.

He tried to get their attention so they might quiet down before being seen by Mr. Brown.

Smokey waved to get the boys' attention. They didn't see him and kept walking toward the front door, which confused him since they never entered the house by the front door. He jumped and waved but they were almost to the door. Smokey was unable to get their attention and they kept right on walking.

Jacob came out the front door and closed it behind him.

Smokey saw the look on Larry's face. He recognized Jacob as the boy with the rifle from the still. They seemed to be sizing each other up: there were three of them and only one Jacob. Smokey couldn't hear them speaking, but he could tell they were exchanging words.

Bob and Sam stood behind Larry as if to say that they were right there if anything happened. They chatted for a few minutes, and then the boys turned to leave. Perhaps Jacob told them that the miner's house belonged to the brothers on Fridays, but during the week it was his gang's and that they better stay out.

Smokey was shocked that they would just walk away without a fuss. The house belonged to the mining company, and they were all trespassers. On the other hand, the unspoken arrangement between the brothers and the other local gangs kept things civil. It was a good arrangement and none of the groups of boys wanted to see that change.

Smokey was glad that they were leaving. He didn't want them involved any more than they already were. However, he also wished he could have their help to get Do What and Ruby free. He was on his own, and he had to figure out what to do to get them loose.

Smokey stood on the log again and peeked inside the window. Do What was still sitting on the chair and Mr. Brown was pacing. The light from the door lit the room as Jacob returned, but when the door closed it went dim again.

He could see the revolver tucked in the back of Mr. Brown's waist. The gun was the biggest challenge to the situation. If Smokey was found, he might be shot. He was so angry at Jacob for turning on them. Smokey vowed that if he got out of this situation alive, he would beat Jacob up. Jacob might be older and bigger, but he would do his best to at least get a few good licks in. Smokey couldn't just stand there and let his best friend be held prisoner. He felt responsible for getting Do What into this situation, and he wanted to get him out.

He had an idea.

He would cause a commotion outside and lure both Mr. Brown and Jacob outside. He would get into the house and lock the front door and untie Do What and escape out the back window as they had done before. It was a long shot, but he had to try something. There wasn't much time. It was late in the afternoon, and it would be harder to do this in the dark. However, the darkness could also be an advantage because he and Do What knew the back roads and trails that could help them escape and hide.

Smokey remembered that there was a coal chute behind the house. Coal deliveries were placed down the chute and into the basement where it would be stored for use in the stove. There was still a large pile of coal dust that surrounded the chute, and he had an idea. He would gather up the coal dust in the nearby bucket and take it to Mr. Brown's car. He would put the coal dust into the tail pipe and stuff it with an old rag he found near the back window. Coal dust is quite combustible. With the right conditions, it could explode. If he could get Mr. Brown's car started, the tail pipe would heat up. He hoped that when the coal ignited, it would cause a decent size explosion that would draw them out of the house.

He carried the bucket of coal dust, careful not to be seen as he walked to Mr. Brown's car. He scooped it into the tail pipe and then shoved the rag inside. He hoped that Mr. Brown had left his key behind so that Smokey could start the car; if not, he would have to try to hotwire the car. Sam was the one who knew how to do that. His older brother Seth showed him how, and the brothers took a few cars joyriding once or twice. He wasn't sure if he knew exactly what to do if he had to hot wire Mr. Brown's car. But, if it came down to it, Smokey would figure it out.

Smokey opened the driver's side door and looked in the sun visor to see if there was an extra set of keys there. Luck was on his side. When he pulled the visor down, a set of keys fell onto the seat. He knew he had to start the car and then run off behind the house because the sound of the car running would draw attention. His plan would only work if both Jacob and Mr. Brown exited the house. He would have only moments to get in and lock the door, free Do What, and get him and Ruby out the back window. This was his only idea, so he needed it to work.

Smokey left the car running and made his way back behind the house, positioning himself near the window with the log ready to climb the moment the car backfired.

A minute passed and no explosion. Two minutes, but still nothing. Smokey was tempted to go see if the car was still idling, but he didn't want to leave his post just in case it finally went off. He stayed perched on the log. The seconds seemed like minutes as he sat waiting for his moment.

After several minutes went by, Smokey knew something wasn't right. The muffler and coal dust should have ignited by now. He had to see what was wrong.

He got down from the log and peeked around the corner. Right in that moment, he saw Sam, Bob, and Larry climbing into Mr. Brown's car. He wanted to shout at them that this was not the car to take for a joy ride. Mr. Brown was not the kind of man to mess with. If he found them, he might shoot them.

The boys slammed the car door shut. Sam peeked out the back window as Larry put the car in drive. He hit the gas and the brothers howled as the car lunged forward. Larry circled the gravel driveway, making a large donut. The boys whooped and hollered while the car continued to gain speed.

Smokey imagined Mr. Brown coming out to find his car hijacked by some local hoods. He could imagine him aiming the pistol and firing at will. He wasn't sure how to handle this situation.

In that moment, the car's tail pipe exploded with coal dust. It gave off a loud boom, resembling a cherry bomb. This would be Smokey's chance. If both Mr. Brown and Jacob came out, he would be set.

He ran to the log and stood up to the window's ledge. He heard the door fly open.

Mr. Brown's voice boomed across the gravel lot.

"What the hell are you kids doing with my car?" he shouted. He rushed from the front porch toward the car, waving his revolver. Smokey saw Jacob run out of the house behind him.

Without wasting any time, Smokey jumped through the window to free Do What and Ruby. He had almost forgotten that he was clinging to the burlap sack that Big Ma gave him, his fist clenched so tightly that the blood vessels in his hand were showing.

Once he pulled himself through the window, he crashed on the floor. He leaped toward Do What to free his hands.

Do What stared at Smokey, surprised.

"Smokey?" he said. Do What watched as Smokey made his way to the door to lock it and get Do What untied. He saw Ruby lying on the floor next to Do What and knelt behind him to untie his hands.

There was so much commotion going on outside that neither Jacob nor Mr. Brown had noticed the door close. He had to act fast if they were going to get out and make it to the trail by the tracks before they discovered that the door was locked and that something was going on.

"Smokey, what are you doing?" Do What asked. He stared at him wide-eyed.

"Getting you and Ruby out of here," Smokey said, untying the last knot to free his friend. He handed him the sack and instructed Do What to put Ruby in there so they could move quickly.

"I can't believe that two-faced Jacob turned you and Ruby over to Mr. Brown," Smokey said, urging them out toward the window.

"Smokey, tie me back up and get out of here," Do What said. The look on Do What's face confused Smokey because Do What seemed to be bothered that Smokey was there at all. He didn't seem a bit grateful that Smokey had created a diversion with the car, with some help from the brothers and snuck in to get him.

"Smokey, you need to get out of here fast," Do What said, sitting back down. "He'll catch you."

"Not if we get out of here. Come on, let's go!" Smokey said. But Do What didn't budge.

"Smoke, you need to leave *now*," Do What pleaded.

Smokey looked at him with confusion. He grabbed the sack, placed Ruby in it, and grabbed Do What's hand to lead him out the window.

Do What pulled back.

"Let's go, Do What," Smokey said.

"No," Do What replied. He sat down again and urged Smokey to leave Ruby and get out while he could.

A gunshot fired and the car sped off down the road as Mr. Brown cursed after it. Smokey peeked out the small crack in the curtain to see what Jacob and Mr. Brown were doing. He heard the door handle being jiggled. There was no time left. Jacob would know something was up and would make his way around the back and in through the window.

Smokey was upset with Do What for not getting up and following him. He didn't understand his reluctance to escape. They would have been home free if he had just listened to Smokey and followed him out the window with Ruby. Now they had Jacob and Mr. Brown to deal with.

Another gunshot.

Smokey stared out the window, wondering if Jacob had already begun to make his way around the house to the back window. When he turned around to check the window, he was surprised to see Jacob standing by Do What with the same coal shovel that Smokey had used to knock him out.

Before he knew it, Jacob swung, and then there was darkness as Smokey was knocked out cold.

When he came to, Smokey found himself lying uncomfortably on the wooden floor of the miner house. His hands and feet were tied behind his back, and his mouth was gagged.

He tried to yell and curse at Jacob, but no sound came out. He looked up at Do What, still tied to the chair, with disdain. Why had he not escaped with him? Why was he seemingly a willing party to Mr. Brown and Jacob?

Next to him on the floor, the sack wiggled and he could hear Ruby whining inside.

He looked around for Mr. Brown but didn't see him. He had no idea how long he had been knocked out, but his head throbbed where the shovel had made contact with his temple.

Mr. Brown entered from the back room and eyed Smokey. He was no longer the kind-eyed man that he met at Lorenzo's boarding house. Now he was a sour and mean man who had nothing but contempt on his face.

"So, are you the little twerp that made my car explode?" Mr. Brown raged, kicking Smokey hard in the gut.

Smokey doubled over in pain. He wanted to get up and punch Jacob for selling them out and for hitting him on the head with the shovel.

"Stop!" Do What said, "Don't hurt him!"

Mr. Brown turned to Do What and slapped him across the face. He said nothing but glared at him for a long time. A tear of anger welled up in the corner of his eye and ran down Do What's face. He stopped protesting.

Mr. Brown turned back to Smokey. "You better hope those little jerks bring back my car in one piece or you will pay."

He kicked Smokey again, this time a little harder. It was impossible to breathe. The wind had been knocked out of him, and he was wincing in pain.

Jacob stepped between Mr. Brown and Smokey.

"Come on, stop! He's had enough," Jacob said.

Mr. Brown's eyes narrowed, and he closed in on Jacob now.

"So, you want to take his licks for him?" he said. He raised his fist as if to belt him.

Jacob raised his fist back.

"Oh, so you want to show you're a man, do you?" Mr. Brown said.

Jacob looked shaken but didn't back down.

Mr. Brown pushed Jacob, taunting him.

"Come on. If you're a man, go ahead, swing," he said. "You're nothing but the son of a washed-up moonshiner that is so pitiful he couldn't even make a living in the mines."

Jacob's nostrils flared. He started to heave and huff, clenching his fists.

"What are you going to do?" Mr. Brown said.

Jacob could take no more. He charged Mr. Brown, tackling him to the ground. They wrestled on the ground.

Jacob finally got the upper hand and pinned Mr. Brown. He swung and punched him square in the nose. They wrestled some more.

"Get him, Jacob!" Do What shouted.

Smokey squirmed on the floor, trying unsuccessfully to free himself. The scuffle continued. Jacob seemed to be winning. Though he was a boy, he was big and strong for his age. He punched Mr. Brown again. Mr. Brown struggled beneath Jacob, attempting to get up, but the boy's weight was enough to keep him pinned to the ground.

Mr. Brown reached for the revolver in his waist. He pulled it out and fired a single shot. Jacob froze with fright and loosened his grip from Mr. Brown. He stared and then fell over, clasping his side. The bullet had hit him, stopping him in his tracks. He groaned in pain.

Do What and Smokey locked eyes in terror.

Do What broke free from his restraints once again. With an intensity Smokey had never seen in his eyes before, Do What lunged for Mr. Brown.

Mr. Brown scrambled to his feet and raised the revolver again. He aimed the gun directly at Do What.

Smokey squirmed and fought to get up to help his friend, but he couldn't. He saw blood flowing from Jacob's side and felt a wave of guilt. He wished he could take back his curiosity. He wished he would have minded his own business. He should have never gotten Do What involved. He couldn't live with himself if Do What got shot too.

Do What faced Mr. Brown, ready to give up his life to defend Smokey.

Mr. Brown turned to aim the gun at Smokey, and Do What froze. It seemed like there would be no way out of this situation.

Suddenly, there was a loud crash at the door. A large man wearing a suit and tie had kicked the door down and stood with his revolver pointed directly at Mr. Brown.

"Drop it, Brown," the agent said.

Mr. Brown dropped the gun. He put his hands behind his back, and the large man handcuffed him.

A moment later, Peter Rose rushed in to help Jacob. He grabbed his handkerchief and held it to Jacob's wound. He turned to Do What.

"Untie Smokey," Peter said. He turned back to the injured boy. "Jacob, I think you're going to be fine," he said. "It grazed your side but didn't penetrate your abdomen."

Just then, Ray and Lorenzo entered the house with the brothers trailing not too far behind them.

Smokey was still sitting on the floor, confused.

"Do What, why didn't you escape with me?" he asked.

Peter stepped forward.

"We've been trying to capture Mr. Brown for some time," he said. "Not just for stealing this dog from the vet in D.C., but for a whole slew of crimes in Maryland. We just needed something bigger than petnapping to put him away for good. The agent tracked him down to Cinder Bottom several weeks ago but didn't have anything to charge him with. But now he can be charged with extortion, kidnapping, and attempted murder. He'll be locked up for a very long time."

"Lorenzo, Ray, you knew?" Smokey said, looking at Ray and Lorenzo.

"We knew," Lorenzo said. "We wanted to keep you out of it, but when you started to ask questions about Mr. Rose, we were afraid that you would figure it out and keep them from getting Mr. Brown."

"And Jacob?" he said.

"Do What and Jacob were used as bait to set up Mr. Brown for kidnapping."

Lorenzo helped Jacob to his feet and helped him to his truck to get him to Doc Henson.

"Do What, you knew too?" Smokey said.

"When you told us to go to Mr. Lorenzo's apartment, the agent was already there."

He went on to explain the plan to Smokey. Jacob was supposed to pretend that he had never left the house. He tied Do What up so they could get Mr. Brown on kidnapping charges. They never thought anyone would be shot. Jacob had to pretend to keep Do What hostage when the agent showed up or they might not be able to arrest him.

Ray stood with his arms crossed. "Smokey, I said stay out of sight behind the house," he scolded and shook his head.

Smokey didn't reply.

Mr. Rose stood and took the little dog from the sack. She whined and licked his face. "This is for Ruby. This little dog is a special gift from the congressman to a young girl named Ruby Bridges in New Orleans, the first black girl to attend an integrated school. She has been under guard by the U.S. Marshals. This dog is a symbol from the nation to young Ms. Bridges for her courage."

Ray reached into his pocket and retrieved the envelope with the stack of ransom money and handed it over to the agent.

At that moment Larry, Sam, and Bob rushed into the house. "Are y'all okay?" Larry asked.

Smokey sat up and gave the "all is well" salute, glancing at Do What. He then reached into his pocket, retrieved what was left of his smashed sandwich, and took a big ol' bite.

"Yep, just fine," he said, and they all laughed.

Sheriff Donnie entered and grabbed Mr. Brown. He escorted him out to the car.

Mr. Brown was arrested on federal charges in Maryland and faced fifteen years in federal prison. The dog was delivered to her new home with Ruby in Louisiana. Jacob recovered well from his gunshot wound and was even given a congressional medal of honor for courage and valor. There was no official ceremony because this was not a sanctioned operation, but he had the medal to prove it.

Do What and Smokey decided that they would stay out of trouble for a while. When they returned to school on Monday, the world seemed like a different place. Like it had shrunk and McDowell County would never be the same.

SMOKEY AND DO WHAT'S ADVENTURES IN CINDER BOTTOM DON'T STOP HERE!

HERE'S AN EXCLUSIVE SNEAK PEEK AT BOOK 2:

GREENBRIER RIVER

Smokey lit his last cigarette. He stood in the cool summer morning waiting for Do What to arrive. He had wanted to get up early enough to have some breakfast before heading down the river to fish, but he was running late. He had made it to the bottom of the holler to meet his childhood friend so they could get some quiet time and fish for the weekend.

He was grateful to be spending the day on the river, but his mind drifted back on the troubles he had left behind at home.

His grandmother had moved in the month before. Her move had been unexpected, and he had not loved the idea of giving up his room. He had only recently inherited the bedroom from his sister. She had moved out, vacating his room, when she married her high school sweetheart. While Smokey thought the man was a donkey of a brother-in-law, he was glad that he had taken his sister away. He would miss her—she was his best friend in many ways—but they had drifted apart ever since she started high school. Her focus had moved outside of the house.

The day was cold, but Smokey was glad the rain had stopped. He wanted nothing more than to relax and enjoy the weekend. He tried not to think about the events of the last week.

He and his friend Larry had gotten into trouble. He liked Larry well enough, but that boy could never let things go. For example, when Smokey had called his girlfriend an angry cow, he could not convince Larry that he was just saying what everyone already knew.

His group of friends, the "brothers," as he called them, didn't back him up. Although they had said the same thing about Betty on many occasions, they just didn't have the guts to say it to Larry's face. She was the worst person in Northfork, and everyone—even Larry—knew it. But he had a hard time finding love, and the fact that a popular girl even would give him the time of day, let alone date him, was all that he could focus on. His lifelong friends and their opinions didn't matter—not anymore. Smokey hated that a girl might break up his band of brothers. He was constantly reminding himself that he was stuck in a world that was limited to the confines of the small town where he was born in.

Smokey was a tall and wiry kid. He looked older than he was, but his innocent face confused his appearance. He was far from innocent, but he used his charm to his advantage. It was as if his boyish charisma, simple brown wispy hair, and calm demeanor didn't matter. When trouble came, he was always in the middle of it.

His dutiful best friend, who was affectionately called Do What, seemed to enjoy his shenanigans. He seemed to long for the next series of trouble that they would encounter.

Smokey was eager for some downtime where he would just throw his fishing line in the water and enjoy a cigarette and a few beers. He never worried about a thing when he was fishing.

Today, he was additionally thrilled to be using Do What's brother's canoe so that they could also travel down the river searching for the best spots to catch smallmouth bass. They would camp along the river, build a fire, and chat into the night about the things that sounded important when you are fifteen (cars, women, and how to get out of their small town).

Both of their fathers had worked in the coal mines. Do What's father had been injured in the mines and hadn't worked in five years. He spent most of his time drinking and throwing fits of rage. His mother worked a few jobs to make ends meet but they didn't have much.

Do What was one of the smartest guys that Smokey knew, not that his school record would reveal that. He was often the last in his class and was a freshman again because he hadn't earned enough credits to pass to the next grade. Not because he was unintelligent, but because he was often daydreaming and thinking of bigger things than a passed test about the Civil War or geometry. He often contemplated what it meant to be alive or whether a man could actually live on the moon. He was a genius if you didn't look at his grades. He was seen as a loser if you talked to his teachers, but Smokey could see beyond the superficial things that those people saw. He saw a brilliant, devoted friend. He knew Do What would stand by him no matter the personal cost.

Smokey hated school, although he was more successful than Do What. The things they taught in school felt like such a waste of time. He found that the things he learned from Harold the bus driver were far more interesting and valuable. Smokey had elected to take vocational courses in Welch, the biggest town in the area next to Bluefield. He hoped to avoid a life working as a coal miner, even though his father and his father before him had been one. Smokey had watched his grandfather suffer and die of black lung, and he knew he didn't want that. He wanted out. Out of Northfork, out of Welch, out of the Bottom.

Smokey was so eager to be an adult that, at times, he forgot he was still a kid. He had been given a lot of responsibility even though he was the baby of the family, the youngest of five kids. One had already died, two were married, and another was headed off to the army in just a few weeks. He was not eager to grow up, just eager to see the world and get out of Appalachia. Though he hated school, he loved to study. He would read books, study maps, and ask the visitors to Cinder Bottom what the world out there was really like. The tales that he heard intrigued him. He wanted to be part of that world and longed for it to come sooner rather than later.

Smokey realized he had been waiting at the holler's bottom for nearly forty-five minutes and grew anxious. Do What was usually on time, but Smokey knew that his friend had to convince his brother to let him use the canoe and also give them a ride upriver so Smokey and Do What could drift back on the river by Sunday evening.

Do What's brother was usually drunk, and this Saturday morning would be no exception. Smokey had hoped that Do What's brother had time to sleep a few hours before having to drive them to the head of the river. He wanted to get the best fishing they could before the late hours of the morning. Do What had promised to do his brother's chores, give him a pack of cigarettes, and a pint of moonshine just for him to agree to drive them. Smokey pitched in money for gas, which he had saved for a week from his tips from his paper route.

Smokey had been looking forward to this trip for weeks. As the minutes ticked by, he grew more worried that Do What's brother had passed out after a night of hanging at the beer joint and forgot about his promise to drive them. It wouldn't be the first time he let down Do What.

One time, he was supposed to pick up Do what from a school field trip in one of the biggest cities in the state, Bluefield, but he was so drunk he had forgotten him. Do What had to hitchhike home and was four hours late.

His brother had been a straight-A student until he was a freshman in high school when his father broke his back in the coal mines. Do What's brother had to get a job working in the mines and dropped out of school to help the family. He was not the same and was often missing for days at a time.

Despite his behavior, Do What always stood up for his brother, even when he beat Do What. Somehow, Do What could see past his brother's struggles. He saw him for the brother he was before everything changed. However, that didn't change how his brother acted, and Do What was cautious about trusting him for anything. But since they didn't have a truck, Smokey had to rely on his friend to get them to the riverhead.

Smokey sat on a log that had fallen on the side of the road. After a while, he lay down and drifted to sleep on the cool spring morning.

He had packed some food, a quilt, and some extra clothes in a plastic bag, to keep them dry in the canoe. He knew that the splashing of the paddles could get his gear wet and didn't want to have wet clothes or bedding. He had packed a small canteen, a flashlight, a cooking pot, his fishing pole, and a hunting knife he took from his brother's toolbox for cleaning the fish he was certain they would catch.

He loved to fish. He found the quiet and the beauty of the river to be intoxicating. Something about being in nature and alone with the elements seemed to spur on his sense of adventure. He loved cooking over an open fire and having to survive in nature alone with his wit and the elements. He imagined he was Daniel Boone, traversing the wild frontier and living off the land. He had also saved up to buy a pack of cigarettes for the trip, which he figured would last the weekend if he didn't chain smoke.

Do What liked to smoke but also didn't do it if Smokey wasn't around. He was not a prude but didn't really think of getting things like moonshine and cig-arettes. He would buy a comic book before cigarettes and a *National Geographic* before moonshine. Do What longed to be in other parts of the world or imagine he was in exotic places like Patagonia or Nepal. His other friends found his constant droning on about these faraway places a bit of a bore and would often leave him off the list of friends they would invite to hang out unless Smokey was around. Smokey was his best friend and often stuck up for his introverted and somewhat eccentric behavior and tastes.

Do What had grown steadily more invisible at home; his brother was always drunk and his father often passed out from his daily consumption of a quart of liquor. His mom worked three different jobs at times to make ends meet—doing laundry for miners and often cleaning houses. Do What was a dutiful son, though he seemed to grow more and more reclusive after his father's accident.

Smokey stirred from his brief nap when he heard a running truck off in the distance. He hoped it was Do What so they could make it down the river before all of the fish stopped biting for the day.

Smokey was tall for his age and had dark brown wispy hair that was slicked back with hair balm. Smokey stood, stretching his long limbs. He smoothed his hair back down.

He could see the reflection from the early morning sun on the top of the underside of the canoe that was strapped to the bed of the truck.

As the truck approached, Do What hung out the side window, waving his baseball cap in a signal of imminent victory. He had somehow managed to get his brother up and out with the canoe.

They pulled over to the side of the road where he stood. Before the truck stopped, the door flung open and Do What hopped out.

"Morning, Smoke," he called.

Smokey gathered his things, flung them in the bed of the pickup, and jumped in after Do What. The car reeked of liquor. The sheer amount of fumes made it hard to breathe. The aftermath of a long night at the beer joint oozed from Mike's pores. He was not talkative and that was fine by Smokey. He was often harsh and rude when sober but often became passive and somewhat pleasant when he was drunk. The fact that he had been out all night and perhaps hadn't gone to bed yet was probably why he was still in this calm mood.

They bounced and slid on the bench seat of the truck as they took the turns in the road at more than the ideal speed. The canoe wasn't tied down well and was sliding back and forth in the bed of the truck. They weren't worried about the canoe, but the screeching sound the canoe made on the bed of the truck became annoying.

"Smokey, check this out," Do What said. He handed him a copy of an old *National Geographic*. "See there, that's the tallest active volcano in Europe, Stromboli. It's right in the middle of the Mediterranean Sea."

Smokey took the magazine from his friend and glanced at the headline. "Visitors Flock to One of the Most Amazing Wonders of the World," it read. He handed it back to his friend.

"That's huge," Smokey said. He was interested, but seeing these exotic places all over the world didn't excite him as much as it made him long for adventure. He wondered what it would be like to sail to that island and hike to the top to see the volcano erupt. He wanted to travel to these places. However, the more he thought about it, the more depressed he got. As much as he struggled against it, some part of himself believed he was stuck in Northfork and would more than likely always be stuck there.

Do What loved to imagine these amazing places, but never thought he would ever go there. He was intrigued by the history and geography of these places. He knew facts, statistics, and lore of many of the countries and small villages he showed to his friend. The pain of seeing them was more than he could bear sometimes, but he couldn't help himself.

Smokey tried to shake off the feeling and focused on the drive. The truck hurled down the road at a breakneck speed and arrived at the head of the Greenbrier River just as the sun began to peek above the ridge. They wished they would have arrived earlier but were grateful that Mike let them use the canoe and gave them a ride, even if that meant that they had to pay in bribes.

The truck pulled to the side of the road. Mike didn't so much as flinch or offer to help unload the canoe. Instead, once they had got their stuff from the truck, he held out his hand for his bounty—the pack of cigarettes and money for his quart of moonshine. Do What handed these over, and Mike sped off back up the road. No words were exchanged, not even goodbye. Do What waved and his brother gave him the bird followed by the flick of his cigarette out of the truck window. The boys shrugged and gathered their things.

Do What had a small bag and a rolled-up blanket tied with some rope to hold it together. They placed their items in the canoe and raised it up over their heads to carry it down to the river's bank.

There was a small fishermen's path that led to the perfect spot to launch the canoe for their adventure. They were both grateful that the canoe survived the winding road and Mike's hectic driving and that they didn't lose the paddles. The aluminum canoe was light, but with their clothes, cooking items, and sleeping gear, they had to be careful not to lose their footing as they carried the boat down the small slope to the shore of the river.

There was something calming about the babbling river edge that put them both at ease. They knew they were going to have a peaceful, quiet time on the river—just them, the fish, and relaxation. It was the perfect weekend, and they were ready to go.

They loaded the canoe, and each boy grabbed a paddle. Smokey held the canoe as Do What made his way to the front.

"Walk in the center and hold on to the sides," Smokey called.

The small canoe began to rock side to side as Do What's large, clumsy feet stumbled into the boat.

"Do what?" he hollered back. He nearly capsized the canoe and lost a paddle before steadying his hands on the sides of the small canoe.

Smokey smiled as he always did when his friend said, "Do what." The nickname fit and, in fact, Do What thought it was funny too. He was a kind soul and could often be seen helping others when he was in need himself.

Smokey wanted to get out of Northfork, away from McDowell County. He wanted to see the world. He often dreamed of taking Do What to see some of these places but stopped mentioning it to him since he knew that Do What would never leave his mom.

Do What sat down and placed his paddle in the water, and Smokey raised the back of the canoe and pushed them off the shore. He stepped effortlessly into the canoe and used the back of the handle of the paddle to push the canoe farther into the center of the river. It was calm and the river flowed gently.

The morning sun began to warm their cold faces. The crisp air was refreshing and the quiet sounds of the morning reminded Smokey of why he loved fishing so much. No cars, no noise, and no worries. The river and fishing were the perfect places to get away from it all.

Smokey had a way of attracting trouble. Not that he would go looking for it, but it would find him. He was curious and that often led to mischief. He certainly didn't run from trouble, but on this trip, he wanted to give trouble a weekend off so he could just relax with his friend.

They didn't have to paddle much to move forward since they were headed with the flow of the river. They just needed to steer and stay in the center away from rocks and the shore.

It was peaceful and they spotted several cardinals. The birds were small, but their beautiful red bodies stood out from the green leaves. They danced in and out of the branches until they eventually disappeared under the canopy of the thick new leaves. In the fall, the color of the leaves made it hard to see them, but the new green growth was a striking contrast to their beautiful feathers.

They paddled for a bit until they arrived at the spot where they wanted to cast their fishing lines. Smokey had already baited his hook with a hellgrammite, a small bug-like animal that looked more like a prehistoric creature rather than an insect. He baited the hooks carefully to avoid the hellgrammite's bite. He hoped that it was enough to catch something for lunch. He prepared the fishing rod for Do What and handed it up to him so they could both fish. They didn't speak much so as not to scare the fish away.

As the sun rose, you could see the small schools of fish come to and from the boat. They were curious. Smokey just hoped they hadn't already eaten their fill of insects. He hoped the fish would bite and that he might get a few nice trout or smallmouth bass, even a catfish or two would make a tasty lunch.

Smokey had first fished in this same spot with his father when he was only eight years old. He had caught many fish there and was certain they would have good luck. He remembered the last time he was there was with his brother, Vernon. He had caught the biggest fish he had ever seen. It was two pounds, and it nearly broke the flimsy rod that his father had ordered from the Sears Catalog. He was proud when that fish fed them all that night. He had a feeling that this spot would bring them luck again.

Do What was not the fisherman that Smokey was. He often splashed his pole into the water when he would drift into thought, or he spoke too loudly and scared the fish, but Smokey enjoyed his company and tolerated the constant questions as much as he could. He had tried to explain to Do What that he had to stay still and quiet, but it seemed as though it would be just minutes before he called out to Smokey to share some facts from his *National Geographic* or turn so swiftly he would shake the boat. The canoe would rock and sway, and Do What would rock and sway as well.

Do What, sometimes oblivious to his size and stature, often tripped over his own feet and stumbled when walking. He was often teased when he was younger because he would walk into walls or trip over rocks. He was always far away, daydreaming, and not focused on what was right in front of him.

Smokey met Do What when he was being teased and Smokey stood up for him. Do What has been loyal ever since, and that happened in elementary school. They spent the summer months having adventures fishing, hunting, and hanging around Cinder Bottom, which was the red-light district of the entire county, perhaps all of West Virginia. You could find brothels, beer joints, moonshiners, and anything else that most places would deem off-limits. Cinder Bottom drew people in from all over the northeast. Those who wanted to indulge and not be questioned or troubled came there. It was the ideal location for people-watching and finding some trouble to get into, which Smokey seemed to attract like flies to honey.

Smokey was always glad to get some quiet time away from the chaotic Cinder Bottom. He found peace in the fresh air and the water.

In the summer months, the river was a bit lower, which made catching fish a bit easier. It was slow and gentle, which made for a smooth float down the river. Early in the morning, there was still a little chill in the air, so until the sun rose above the tree line it was cold and Smokey wished he had a cup of coffee. He had brought some to make for breakfast, but the late start meant it was too late to make a fire.

To take away the chill, Smokey lit his cigarette, a Pall Mall. The taste quenched his thirst for coffee and put him into a relaxed state, which is just what he wanted. He knew that the only time he could smoke was when he was away from home. His pa didn't mind that he drank beer or liquor but didn't want him to smoke.

Some of his friends used to tease him that that's how he got his name. "Smoking since birth," they would say to him. The truth was that he was born a blue baby and they didn't know if he would live. One of his Pa's friends told his parents his name should be Smokey and that stuck, even though his given name was Curtis. His mother loved that name and used it stubbornly. But Smokey stuck and everyone else called him that.

Do What would smoke on occasion but often would forget that he had a cigarette hanging from his mouth and would not even smoke it. He was prone to daydreaming. Often the lit cigarette would burn his lip without him ever taking more than a single puff.

Smokey offered him a cigarette, but this time Do What passed, which was fine with Smokey. That meant he could have one more before lunch, which made him smile.

They found the spot where Smokey was certain they'd find calm water and biting fish, but there didn't seem to be as many fish as he remembered from before. He wanted to catch another two-pounder but knew that he would have to be patient if he wanted to catch anything that morning. Smokey was often anxious when he didn't get at least a bite before the sun rose above the trees. He could feel the air warming, and he knew that if they didn't catch something soon, they would have to move to a different spot on the river. They would need to find somewhere shady, a spot where the sun didn't expose the fish, and the fish needed to take a risk on a nibble of hellgrammites.

Do What was so engrossed with his *National Geographic* magazine that he didn't notice the line on his fishing pole begin to bounce. He had a nibble. Then all of a sudden, the pole bent in half and nearly went into the water. Do What was still oblivious until Smokey shouted for him to catch the rod.

Smokey was a little bothered that Do What had a bite and had not even been trying. He had been casting his line and spying the perfect casting spot for his line. Do What quickly sprung to life, grabbed the fishing pole, and began to reel it in.

"Don't jerk it. Take it easy!" Smokey shouted. Do What carefully reeled in the line, and Smokey made his way to the middle of the canoe with the net to bring in the haul. Do What pulled and reeled in for what seemed like an eternity as if he was bringing in Moby Dick himself. The pole bent and wiggled as the fish neared the surface.

"Don't lose him!" Smokey hollered.

"I won't!" Do What called back. The fish made it to the surface and began to thrash. The last yank from Do What's pole sent the fish into the air, headed right for Smokey. Like catching a fair ball in the outfield, Smokey dove forward and caught the fish in the net. The boys cheered as if he had just caught the final out of the world series. It was a beautiful bass, probably over a pound and a half. They were both proud and they put it in a bucket of water they had for their prize booty.

Satisfied that they had exhausted the fishing in that spot, they made their way down the river. The sun was shining on the water now. The light danced along the small ripples on the river and made the water sparkle. The morning air began to warm their cold bones and they found a nice place to pull on shore to enjoy some lunch. They decided to build a small fire and enjoy their catch.

Do What wasn't fond of gutting fish, but Smokey had been taught by his father how to gut the fish, remove the scales, and filet it so they could cook it over the fire.

Smokey loved eating fresh fish, especially when he caught it himself. He felt a little jealous of Do What, but the grin on Do What's face made those feelings fade. This was the only fish his friend had ever caught.

The last time they went fishing, Do What had almost caught one of the biggest catfish that Smokey had ever seen. Do What had been so distracted with his world atlas that he hadn't even noticed that a fish was on his line. The fish was so big, in fact, that it had leaped from the water with the bait in its mouth.

When Do What had finally noticed and tried to pull it in, the fish pulled the rod right out of his hand. What had to have been the biggest catfish in the Greenbrier River vanished. Smokey had beat himself up for not noticing sooner. He wondered if he could have saved the fish.

Do What forgot about the whole thing moments after it happened and returned to his reading. For Smokey it was not so easy to forget, but he forgave Do What's lackadaisical behaviors.

Today, he was glad that he was able to help rescue lunch and catch it in the net. Smokey was glad that this day was different.

TO OUR DAD, SMOKEY,

There are so many things I could write about our dad, Smokey, and how much he inspired us to write these stories. His passion for storytelling and his belief in the importance of life and love were the driving forces behind this book. We are forever grateful for his influence and the stories he shared with us.

Dad gave us a glimpse into what life was like when he grew up in the hollers of Northfork, West Virginia. The stories and his perspective were so unique of the communities in that part of Appalachia. Throughout his life, he watched the area rise and fall economically and socially. It's like Dad got to see it toward the high points and also the big decline.

He grew up near a red-light district named Cinder Bottom, in a place misunderstood by most of the world outside of McDowell County. Dad saw the good in people and also got to see the wild side of coal mining communities where corruption, gambling, and prostitution were kept in business for decades in a remote and hidden place in the mountains of southern West Virginia.

ABOUT THE AUTHORS

STEVE VANNOY was born to Curtis "Smokey" and Peggy Vannoy, and he was raised in Bluefield, West Virginia. As a grandson, nephew, and cousin of several coal miners throughout Appalachia, Steve gained a unique perspective into the history of McDowell County,  where both of his parents were born and raised. His love of West Virginia and its rich history from an early age led him to become a winner of the "Golden Horseshoe" award. Steve's mission in writing these stories is to preserve the life and community light on the place called home tucked in between the hills and hollows of southern West Virginia.

Trained as an industrial engineer at West Virginia University, Steve worked in various industries across the state. He is the cofounder of an award-winning publishing company and spends his time with his partner, his family, and their two adorable pups.

AZUL TERRONEZ is a *Wall Street Journal* and *USA Today* bestselling author. His TEDx talk, *What Makes a Good Teacher Great*, has been viewed over 4 million times.

This is his second novel, and he is proud to share his partner's love for West Virginia.

He spends his time writing books, coaching authors, and telling stories from the stage. He splits his time between Santa Cruz, California, and Portugal. When not writing, he is spending time with his family and playing with his rambunctious dogs.

If you enjoyed Smokey and Do What's
first Adventure in Cinder Bottom,
please leave a **REVIEW** on Amazon.

Follow along as their story continues at
CINDERBOTTOM.COM

Thank you!